BOY IN THE BLUE HAMMOCK

BOY IN THE BLUE HAMMOCK

A NOVEL

DARREN GROTH

NIGHTWOOD EDITIONS

1 2 3 4 5 — 26 25 24 23 22

Nightwood Editions
P.O. Box 1779
Gibsons, BC V0N 1V0
Canada
www.nightwoodeditions.com

COVER DESIGN: TopShelf Creative
TYPOGRAPHY: Carleton Wilson

Canada
Canada Council for the Arts
Conseil des Arts du Canada
British Columbia Arts Council
British Columbia

Nightwood Editions acknowledges the support of the Canada Council for the Arts, the Government of Canada, and the Province of British Columbia through the BC Arts Council.

This book has been produced on 100% post-consumer recycled, ancient-forest-free paper, processed chlorine-free and printed with vegetable-based dyes.

Printed and bound in Canada.

LIBRARY AND ARCHIVES CANADA CATALOGUING IN PUBLICATION

Title: Boy in the blue hammock / Darren Groth.
Names: Groth, Darren, 1969- author.
Identifiers: Canadiana (print) 20210396717 | Canadiana (ebook) 2021039675X | ISBN 9780889714267 (softcover) | ISBN 9780889714274 (EPUB)
Classification: LCC PS8613.R698 B69 2022 | DDC C813/.6—dc23

For W, for C, and especially for J. You made these words—
I just wrote them down.

1

Third glass of red in hand, I turned on the TV and watched the fallout of the election.

A crowd in face masks, praying at a cemetery.

A lone teen on an unnamed street corner, throwing rocks at a Reparation Party banner.

A woman shouting into the camera, grasping it with both hands, crying.

Five minutes was enough to give me heartburn. I belched and scanned the program guide. So many voyeurs and their exclamation marks: "Decision Aftermath!" "The Bitter Road Ahead!" "A Nation Divided!" I switched to a sitcom I'd seen dozens of times. The laugh track was my cue to drink.

"Everyone asleep but us," I said.

Tao, laying on the rug, stretched and wagged his tail.

"You're settling in well. Except for almost killing yourself Wednesday. Didn't know gum was poisonous, did you? And toothpaste? Me neither. We need to keep you safe and secure when we go out."

He blinked as I pointed a finger.

"You're not supposed to be here. You were meant to be in service. Helping someone… less fortunate." I uncrossed my legs and leaned forward, elbows digging into my thighs, drink clasped in my interlocked hands. "But you weren't up to it."

Staring at the brown blanket lying in a heap on the floor, I raised my glass.

"Join the club, pup."

First light finds the entrance to the townhouse. Small disturbances dot the scene: the *Starry Night* print askew on the wall, the welcome mat kicked sideways, the potted succulent knocked over on the shelf above the coat rack. Minor disorder. Modern life's bumps and thumps.

The front door holds irrefutable evidence of home invasion: the door bulges in the middle, a belly of splintered cedar and chipped paint. The doorknob hangs limply from its socket.

*

Tao, lying at the foot of the stairs, begins to stir. The fug in his nostrils pushes back onto his tongue. In his throat, the cluster of smells separates.

Rubber. Diesel. Silicone. Cordite.

He doesn't know the names but he senses their meaning, what they've brought to his home.

*

He is tied to the handrail at the foot of the stairs. The lead securing him—a tattered length of polyester, plain on one side, patterned bones and paw prints on the other—runs across his overturned water dish, loops back through a jackboot print on the floor then snakes over the carpeted step to attach at his collar.

Tao is not unfamiliar with constraint. Any time Family leaves the house, he is secured, harmful temptations out of reach.

Family hasn't left the house—they are upstairs. He must get to them. He must be with them. Tao knows this better than he knows his own addled mind.

*

He lifts his head, dips it to the right. Stares at the red, coin-sized patch on his paw. His skin howls. The allergies that factored into his dismissal from the training program chew on him as if he were a new toy. Legs. Ears. Chest. Eyes. The pain reminds him of the stabs of a blackberry bush, but not just when you brush past it or step on it. The thorns are inside, under the hair, pressing on muscles, digging into bones.

Tao sniffs his paw, licks it once. The angry red coin settles for a few seconds, then surges back, vibrating and smug. He is tempted to put his paw between his teeth and bite down—fight fire with fire—but he knows that surrender means being lost for a time.

He won't surrender, not when time is so precious.

He shifts onto his front elbows, gathering his legs under him to stand. Pain grips his lower body, knocking him back onto his haunches. For several seconds, he is dazed. Is this a punishment? He opens his mouth, allowing his tongue to loll, then looks back over his shoulder.

The hip and knee of his right hind leg are out of their usual alignment. The paw is at an unnatural angle, pointing toward the wall opposite the stairs. It carries a gnawing throb Tao can hear as well as feel. He considers the crooked limb for a moment. How did it happen? When? His last memory is of the hounds, breaking the door open, dragging him across the floor, tying him to the stairs, needling his neck. Then the memory fades to black.

*

Get to them.

Be with them.

*

Tao swallows, pants. Swallows again. Favouring his left side, he manages to stand. He looks back; the injured leg hovers just above the carpet, resisting gravity, bearing no weight. The pain is manageable, a scolding pulse rather than a volcanic scream. He turns back and considers the lead fixing him to the stairs.

He leans back. The collar settles into the fleshy base of his ears. He plants his left rear paw, nails digging for extra purchase. Summoning every working muscle, Tao braces, then extends, throwing his ninety-pound frame back and down. The leash strains and the collar chokes. A squall of white noise rages in his skull. Amidst the storm, he waits for reward: an inch of give, then the release. It doesn't come. The jaws of the restraint hold firm. After seven seconds, with small grey blotches staining his vision, Tao stops pulling and eases himself down.

He tries twice more, the efforts producing nothing beyond heat and weight and tiny whimpers and drops of urine.

Readying for a fourth attempt, he hears the only sound that could distract him from his purpose.

Faint, faraway. But budding, growing.

A siren.

The hounds. Coming again. To break more bones, darken more memories.

Tao understands he won't survive a second attack. So be it—he has nothing left now but sorrow and pain and appetite. And a final duty. As soon as it is fulfilled, he is ready to die.

*

Get to them.

Be with them.

*

He closes his eyes, letting his mind break free as it does when he is dreaming. A thread, grey in colour, floats down from the ceiling. It lands on his back, attaching itself to his golden coat. One thread becomes two, then four, then eight. Strands stitch and intersect. Cloth clings and spreads. Soon, Tao is covered from shoulders to rump.

Stone-grey body. Royal blue trim. Stamp of the program.

The training jacket.

At first glance, it is the uniform he failed, the destiny he fumbled. This presence is something else though. Something deep. Something found. A potential somewhere between reality and fantasy. His muscles respond, lengthening. Fibres twitch and fizz. Striations tremor like live wires. The noises camped in his head—the hiss of inflamed skin, the growl of a broken leg—shrink down to mere specks. He is twice his normal size now, a hulking beast for whom restraint is nothing more than pesky annoyance, like fleas in the fur.

The siren continues to wail, looming large, closing in. It is fuel—no longer a clarion of fear. Tao coils and crouches. The world is consumed by the voice of Trainer:

Come

Follow

Hup-up

Tao flings himself backwards. The room shakes. Walls fracture. The floor is a bed of burning coals. For a moment, he is a tug-of-war, his giant frame tearing at the seams. Then the collar on his neck explodes. He flies, just long enough to understand that glorious freedom comes with a steep price. A seismic *whump* rocks the air as the dog crashes into the wall behind.

Tao's whirling senses wane and settle at the foot of his mind. He pants for a moment, then sniffs at a sweater dislodged from the coat rack and half-draped over his prostrate haunches. It smells of hand soap. It belongs to Boy. He noses it aside as the gavel of his broken leg returns, banging in his ears. He stares at the rail. The leash lies bundled on the floor like an abandoned snake skin.

The jacket has vanished.

The siren is retreating.

Tao's jowls draw back, exposing his teeth and releasing his tongue. He will get to them. He will be with them. He gathers, stands on three good legs and limps toward the upstairs bedrooms.

2

"You weren't around for the diagnosis," I said. "How do you think I handled it?"

Tao, snout resting on my bare feet, opened his eyes.

"You're right, pup. Not great."

It didn't matter that I'd known something was… different… for a while. God, more than a while—I'd known from the first few months. The diagnosis though, the actual words on paper… It was like gravity gave out and I was floating away. I didn't know what it meant, I didn't know what to do. I was scared.

I flicked through pages of the old photo album.

Hospital gowns.

Incubator.

Milk.

Baths.

Sleeping together.

Sleeping apart.

Birthday cake.

Toys.

Playgrounds.

Piggybacks.

Smiles. Always smiles.

Jay immediately went into fix-it mode. Told me everything would turn out okay. Things could be a lot worse. Thirty years ago, they knew nothing. Less than nothing. They thought the parents were to blame, especially the mother. These days, people understood more. There was help, money. Medicine. The future was bright for kids like Kasper. Who knew? Maybe there'd be a breakthrough in our lifetime?

I abruptly shut the album. The clap made Tao jump.

Jay had said we were lucky to have our boy. And the world of tomorrow was only going to get better.

I pressed the album to my chest and looked out of the back door. The Benitez house to the right of the big cherry tree was dark and empty, as it had been since the start of the nightly patrols.

At the top of the stairs is a small wooden stand with two shelves. The lower shelf, crammed with boxes of beads and thread and tracing paper, has never held any interest for Tao. Not so the upper shelf; it has, at different times, housed tufts of rabbit fur, sheets of deer hide, nests of eagle feathers. A smorgasbord calling.

He answered only once. The temptation: a moccasin, one of a handmade pair. He found it one morning on the floor, fallen from the shelf. A gift from the gods. He was reluctant to eat it—he understood that it belonged to Woman, that it meant something to her. He could smell her in the hide, lingering scents her hands had left behind. But Woman's imprint was no match for genetic weakness emboldened by primeval instinct. When he was done, he was satisfied to find the centrepiece—an intricate wattle tree months in the making, fashioned from tiny beads of green and gold—had been left untouched.

Today the upper shelf houses, as it has for the past month, large swaths of moose hide. Tao limps past. No pause, no turn of the head, no sniff of the stand. He rounds the corner and is confronted with the door to Woman and Man's bedroom. It is ajar. He noses it open. The door arcs away, striking the dresser, then settling at a forty-five-degree angle with the threshold.

*

Clothes and books are strewn about the floor. The lamp from Woman's bedside table is lying by the wardrobe, surrounded by glass from a broken light bulb. The window nearest the closet is cracked, the fissure like a lightning bolt captured and preserved. A black and white photo of Family has fallen from the wall and is wedged in behind the headboard of the bed.

Tao notes the two large suitcases in the room. The one on Man's side of the bed is laid flat, open, empty; the other is in the corner, listing against the wall, half-unzipped, clothes spilling out as if disgorged. The dog makes his way around to Woman's side of the bed. He sits, careful to lean away from his injured leg, and digs at his itchy inflamed ear. He surveys the length of Woman's body. She is lying on her back, concealed from the waist down. At the bottom of the blanket, one of her feet is exposed, the turquoise-painted nails like a string of tiny planets set in the deep space of the jet-black footboard. Tao waits a few moments, then pushes off from his healthy paw, lifting his upper body onto the bed.

A pillow is covering Woman's face. He nudges it with his nose. The smell is familiar, but flecked with the sour trace of a stranger's hand. Tao takes the corner of the pillowcase in his teeth and eases the pillow aside. He waits again before stretching forward and licking Woman's ear. No shying away. No wiping the slobber. No thank you for the kisses. Tao pushes his pink nose into her cheek; the skin is cold and dry, bereft of the softness he's known for five years. He whines—a small, jagged *nmph*—as he pivots off the bed and makes his way back to the open side.

Man's long, lean arm has escaped the blanket and hangs over the edge of the mattress, the hand closed in a weak fist. Two fingers and the thumb are caked with dried blood. Ignoring the gurgles and moans of his stomach, Tao nuzzles Man's hand. Its rigidity reminds him of the plastic dolls Girl would throw into the yard and get him to fetch.

He lays down, sits his jowly chin between his paws and closes his eyes. He wills the jacket to return, to give him strength. He waits, ears primed, tail ticking side to side. No response, bar a breath of wind nudging the curtain and rattling the warped screen in the window.

Tao stands. He nuzzles the stiff hand of Man a second time then steps back through the clothing and the books, heading for Girl's room.

*

The evidence of violence is subtle: a mirror chipped, a hinge bent. A ballerina music box pulled apart and dumped on the dresser. A toy bear with all its limbs removed. Tao is sure about these small devastations. The big one, he initially questions.

Girl is lying in a familiar pose: on her stomach, head turned toward the door. Her large brown eyes are open, blue-streaked hair tucked behind her ear. The pillow is under her cheek. She's smiling. As Tao edges closer, he anticipates her voice. A sweet hello or maybe a bark of rebuke, in case he has designs on stealing a crayon or a stray sock or, his favourite, a used tissue. He loves her voice. He loves *her*. He has loved her since the first night he came to stay, when she snuck him carrots under the dinner table and lay with him on the floor whispering secrets in his ear.

He arrives bedside. The smile is a lie. Girl's stretched mouth and parted lips are a mask, moulded in the jump-cut between shock and terror. He whimpers, then looks around the room. A source of their occasional wrestling matches—a duck minus its beak, squeaker and most of its stuffing—is half buried beneath a teetering pile of old sketch pads. He takes the duck in his mouth, then gives it to Girl, nestling it in the crook of her bent elbow.

Back out in the hallway, Tao drops his head and vomits on the carpet. Emptying the meagre contents of his stomach brings some clarity, if not relief. The first part of his vow—get to them—is complete. And with the awful truth confirmed, he can now fulfill his promise in its entirety. He will go back into Woman and Man's room and, ignoring the cold foot and the stiff hand, he will curl up on his corner bed for a day, a week, a year, however long it takes for the sirens to fill the air and the hounds to bring their eternal darkness.

Tao steps toward what he expects will be his final resting place, then stops. He feels an itch. Not the usual sting of sensitive skin; this is a deeper irritation, one that gnaws on his bones. It won't be soothed with a scratch or a bite or a vigorous shake of the head.

He turns to face the third bedroom.

Boy.

Tao stares at the door.

He can't see the sky-blue paint, can't recognize the absence of a lock, can't read the wooden block letters carefully arranged and pinned with tacks:

K-A-S-P-E-R

I-S

I-N

Tao knows this door is different, though. So, too, what's beyond the door. The bed, the furniture. The books and the toys. The smells.

And Boy.

Boy is different.

Tao knew this from their first contact. Tao was a visitor then, a guest in Family's house at nights and on weekends. Woman introduced them, cautioning Boy to be gentle. Boy's frame was much smaller than today, but still thin. Skin had fewer freckles. Approaching Tao, Boy had made a noise—a low hum that started in the belly—and touched Tao's ear with the tip of an index finger. Then leapt back, looking at the finger through half-closed eyes and laughing. It was their only physical contact in the first week of the billet.

Tao stares. The room need not be entered to know the scene. If Woman, Man and Girl couldn't resist the hounds, then Boy was easy prey. And, truth be told, Tao doesn't want to observe more loss, though this loss would mean less than the others.

The itch, though. Pressing. Kneading. Issuing a command that must be obeyed.

The dog bows his head, licks the red blotch on his paw. His tail curls under his hips, a question mark without the tittle.

He enters.

*

Against the northern wall, a double bunk. The top bed, vacated by Girl five years ago, carries a box of assorted Playmobil figures and a special edition hardback of *The Gingerbread Man*. Opposite the bunk beds is a small table, its painted-purple surface displaying words neatly written in black Sharpie: *APPLE, SEVEN, MOM, YELLOW, KASPER, PLEASE.* The night light burns as though trying to match the sunshine streaming through the dusty blinds. Piles of Lego dot the floor, the mounds like plastic anthills. On the southern wall, a map of Gilder—village, farms, roads, parks, hospital, schools.

The room is controlled chaos.

Undisturbed.

Tao sniffs a small harmonica on the carpet beneath the bunk bed's ladder, then sits. He stares at the hammock hanging from a hook on the ceiling. Boy is inside—Tao can tell by the hammock's teardrop shape. Boy climbed into the hammock on most days, often with Woman or Man standing by. If the moment was happy or calm, Boy would lay down and stretch, hands and feet leaking out the edges. Swing and make noises and laugh. Sing songs: "The Wheels on the Bus," "You've Got a Friend in Me." Boy would stay for hours, until hunger sparked a quest downstairs for a bowl of cereal or a box of rice crackers. If the moment was *difficult*—a word Woman used from time to time—retreat was favoured over advance. Boy would curl into a ball, turning the knuckles and the knees white. Cry and shout. Scream. Maybe laugh; not the full-throated, joyous hoot of a time not difficult, but a staccato giggle that saw the hands shake under the command of an unkind puppeteer.

Tao leans in and nudges one of the folds in the blue polyester. The hammock turns slowly, clockwise, then counter. Tao puts his nose on the round bulk and pushes. The hammock eases forward, back. The knotted rope creaks as it writhes against the metal hook. There is no other sound, no movement inside the teardrop.

Tao yawns and exits the room.

He never understood why this soft, vulnerable breed occupied a special rank in Family. Boy should've been the lowest in the pack and, yet, ate with everyone else, sometimes before the others had begun. The food, made separately from the main meal, was plentiful. Boy never had to wait for permission to take a place on the couch. When the five of them went out together, he walked in step rather than behind.

One time, Tao challenged the error. Sitting on the living room rug together, Boy reached for the tennis ball lying between them. Tao bared his teeth and growled, the message clear: know your place, understand what you are. The result, though, fell short of the desired dominance. Boy paused but didn't withdraw. Blinked. Tilted the head to one side. Produced frog-like sounds from a slightly open mouth. There was nothing in Boy's face and body that Tao wished to see: no deference, no apology, no fear.

The fear belonged instead to Woman. She shouted and shook her finger and grabbed the baggy skin on the back of Tao's neck. She flung open the back door and cast him out into the courtyard. It didn't matter that it was snowing outside, or that he hadn't eaten. He remained in exile until the snow turned to rain and the rain gave way to sun. Until he knew his place, understood what he was.

There are no places now. No order. Only a final measure of loyalty. And there is no doubt as to where loyalty ultimately lies. As he limps once more across the threshold of Woman and Man's room, he is positive the hounds killed Boy first.

Avoiding eye contact with the masters' motionless bodies, Tao lays down on his bed. He sighs, puts his head between his paws and, before the next gust of wind rattles the warped screen in the window, he is asleep.

*

He dreams about a time four and a half years ago when moments of joy and laughter were still plentiful, before bans and lockdowns and war zone streets, before unease settled permanently in the house like a stubborn stray.

At first, the scene is true to memory. They are at the lake. The sun shines down from a forever sky and the water, though cool, is irresistible. The cedars lining the far bank shrug and nod in the gentle spring breeze. Tao, swimming with the fevered, near-frantic paddle innate to his breed, is in a moment of delicate balance. He is euphoric, playing with Family, surrounded by shrieks of delight, raw skin soothed by the lake's crisp touch. He is also anxious; the water is deep and he is adrift, unsure of where his feet can find solid ground again. As the current picks up, the balance is disturbed. The pack climbs onto a pontoon twenty metres from the water's entry, first Girl, then Man and Woman. Boy is last, but there is no concern—a vault out of the green wash and onto the feet without a hint of helping hand.

Tao is alone in the water.

In the true memory, he is not forgotten—Woman watches his restless approach, then, at the cusp of the platform, she cradles his haunches to aid a scramble onto dry land. In the dream, there is no such rescue.

The harder he swims, the more the pontoon remains out of reach. He yelps and barks, hoping to alert Family to his struggle. They stand backs turned, facing the far bank, oblivious to his plight. His desperate paddling starts to falter. Water enters his mouth, throat, lungs. He sinks, darkness enveloping him. Stars on the surface of the lake flicker, then wink into nothing.

*

Tao wakes. Noises. Footfalls. Creaking floorboards. Shifting carpet. The huff of a door opening, the soft bump as it touches the wall. No siren, though. No surprise—Tao knows the presence of the hounds isn't always announced.

He has no fear. He remains on his bed, head between his paws, unmoved. Where he wants and needs to be. He exhales through his nose and blinks twice. The end has come and he is content, duty done. Even his skin is a tranquil garden.

The expected enemy appears at the entrance to Woman and Man's bedroom. Tao lifts his head, cocks it to one side. The pack he'd been anticipating—it is elsewhere. The figure at the threshold is alone.

It isn't a hound.

3

We watched the march cross in front of the car. Fewer protesters than the previous week. The fewest to date. Placards tilted left and right. Some rested on shoulders. Far fewer held high in clenched fists. The police looked on. And others new to the fray, wearing brown uniforms with bold badges, letters in all caps on their backs: HOMELAND UNION SECURITY HQ.

"We're sitting here doing nothing," I said.

"We're raising a family."

"There are families out there."

"They don't have a disabled child."

"Regardless, we should be fighting."

"I am fighting."

"You are?"

"Every day." Jay turned the car away from the straggly line of resistance. "I'm fighting to... not... think."

In my side mirror a clutch of the brown uniforms confronted a woman carrying a effigy at the front of the march. "To not think?"

"Yes."

"Is that wise?"

"It's essential."

"So, you just want to pretend everything's fine with the world?"

Jay looked in the rear-view, confirming the scene in the back seat. The kids asleep, heads leaning toward each other as if magnetic. Like this, you could imagine them as bookends.

"The world can take care of itself," he said. "Our son can't. All the thoughts that go along with it... that's what I'm fighting." He turned the wheel. Passing St. Mark's and its most recent sign gone viral—"We Are Better Than This"—he recalled the admission his brother had once made to him: "The times I am clean, I allow myself to think about getting wasted for five minutes a day. The other twenty-three hours and fifty-five minutes, I fight to not think about getting wasted."

"That's me," he said. "Five minutes a day. I think about things I'm shit-scared of for our boy. Meltdowns in the middle of the street. Bullies. Getting lost. Ending up homeless, wandering the streets. To name a few. Then I think about the things he doesn't understand, will never understand. He'll never be

independent. Never have a partner. Never have kids. Mom will die one day. Dad will die one day. Gab will die one day. He'll die one day. I think about all of it for five minutes. Then I fight."

Jay wiped his eyes with the knuckle of his index finger. I offered him a tissue from the glove compartment. He waved it away and I dabbed at my own tears.

"I know what those people back there are saying. I know what's making them take to the streets. The country is going down a bad path, a scary path. For our children's sake we can't let it happen. We need to turn it around for them. And those people back there—they will win. Fear has a shelf life." He pulled into the driveway. Killed the engine then ran a hand through his thinning hair. "Not so for our boy. The world won't ever turn around for him. The world was scary from the moment he opened his eyes. It was beyond his comprehension the day his words died."

He got out, opened the passenger door and kissed our still-sleeping son on the forehead. As he lifted the limp body into his arms, he murmured, "My five minutes is up."

"Kasper.

"Kasssssper.

"Once there live Kasper.

"Once there live Kasssssper."

Kasper opens his mouth to speak again, pauses, then taps his thigh. In his right hand, he holds the hardback of *The Gingerbread Man*. Draped across his shoulders is a brown blanket. He wears yellow headphones. He stands on tiptoe.

*

Tao stares, unsure if Boy is real or conjured from his dream. He looks toward the bed. If Boy has risen from the dead—it must be so; if this were a dream, the mossy smell of the lake would be apparent—then perhaps the masters will rise too?

He shifts his gaze, from Woman to Man, again to Woman. No change to their stillness. Tao turns back to Boy, whimpering.

*

"Made the shape.

"Made the shaaaaape.

"Currans for eyes.

"Cherry for nose."

Kasper lets the book slide from his hand and onto the floor. Three steps. A half dip, a jump. Soon, he is at his destination: the window with the rattling screen. He places a finger against the mesh and brings his right hand up close to his mouth. The finger lifts and the rattle is gone. He pulls on the left headphone, lets it snap back against his ear.

He shuffles toward the bed, gaze fixed on the framed family photo wedged behind the headboard. He steps over the pillow on the floor and, with a strength belying his thin stature, reefs the frame free. For several seconds, he holds the photo close, the glass almost touching his nose. Then he extends his arms—past the headboard, past the frozen features of his mother—and slips the frame back onto its hook.

Standing once more beside the bed, he wipes his dusty hands down the front of his shirt and points at the picture.

"Mommy... Daddy... Kasper... Gabrielle...

"My family...

"Deep breaf... huuuuuh...

"Deep breaf... huuuuuh..."

Through narrow, averted eyes, Kasper scans the scene in the bed. He picks up a pair of glasses from the floor, wipes them on his sleeve and places them on Mom's face, ensuring the frame is straight and fitted over the ears. He wraps his arms around her discoloured neck.

"No sleeping... No wake..."

After a full minute, he stands up straight. He feels a scream building in his chest, the kind of choking shriek his classmate Patrick Brough would release when he had to use a public washroom. Kasper slaps his sternum five times. Then he wipes his eyes and makes his way to the other side of the bed.

There is a fly on Dad's arm. Kasper claps his hands then rears back as the fly lifts off and buzzes out into the hallway. He scours the room, making sure there are no other bugs. Then, rocking to and fro on the balls of his feet, he returns his focus to his father. He touches the shaved head, the full beard. Rests his forehead against Dad's cheek.

The bulging eyes—Kasper doesn't look at them.

*

Tao readies to move, then stops. He watches Boy climb onto the bed and squeeze into the small gap between Woman and Man. He has seen them together in bed like this many times; after the sirens became inescapable, it might've been every day. Tao returns to his mat. It is good that he is not alone in honouring the fallen masters.

He is readying to sleep when he senses a shift in Boy. Sideways looking at him. Sitting up, climbing over Woman's legs, stepping onto the floor. Walking toward him on tiptoes.

*

"Poor fing…

"Poor fing…"

Kasper settles beside the left front shoulder of Tao. He sits, crosses his legs, jabs his left hand into the waistband of his jeans. A sound like flapping wings skitters from his pursed mouth. At the window, the curtains shift. Strains of faraway shouting followed by a *pop-pop-pop* seep into the room. The warped screen judders again. Kasper isn't bothered this time—his focus is reserved for the family pet that has largely remained a stranger during their five years together. He places his right hand above the dog's head, palm down, as if bestowing a blessing. Taking care not to touch, he runs his hand down the neck, along the spine, until he arrives at the misshapen back leg.

Kasper frowns. Though he leans forward for a closer inspection of the damage, his hovering hand stays put. A small twitch finds the tip of his pinky finger.

"Oh, noooo… Poor fing…

"Poor fing."

*

Instinct tells Tao to back away. He has seen Boy inflict pain. It is a hunger, not unlike his own appetites to fill his yawning stomach and quell his fiery skin. One taste, one bite… It is never enough.

But Boy never fed on others—only himself. In all their days together, Tao observed only self-harm. A bumped head led to three quick slaps at the site of the blow. A bad meal saw fists gouge deep into a distended belly. A gashed leg instigated fingernail scrapes until Man and Woman held Boy's wrists and Girl pressed a towel to the bloody wound. At no time has another suffered at the hands of Boy.

The dog knows these incidents are in the past, when life was predictable and understood, and the actions of humans made sense. Now the world is a tornado, and suffering at the hands of others is its eye. Perhaps with Family gone, Boy wishes to share his pain?

Tao watches the palm poised over his damaged leg, then turns his attention to the face. The usual displays—the tics, the twists, the twitches—they're absent. In their place is a silence the dog has rarely before encountered. And a resolve; in the eyes, in the set of the jaw. He leans in, intending to lick Boy's arm. He misses, swiping only the acrid air with his tongue.

*

Kasper gets to his feet, taps out a quick march on his thigh and, after collecting his blanket, walks toward the door. At the threshold, he bows his head. *The Gingerbread Man* lies next to his left foot, the pages awkwardly bent under the weight of the splayed cover. He picks up the book, smooths out the creases. As he exits, he speaks in a low voice that comes from deep inside his chest.

"Smiley mouth...

"Free buttons on shirt...

"Into the oven...

"Outoo the garden..."

*

After Boy rounds the corner, Tao swallows the meagre strands of saliva in his dry mouth and sits up. His stomach shudders. The crimson sores on his body cry out. His busted leg beats like a snare drum.

The itch has returned, deeper, louder. It speaks now. The voice of Trainer with new commands.

Lead

Lead him

Out

Away

Tao stares at the picture of Family that Boy replaced on the wall. Defiant order amidst the chaos.

Far away

From wrecked doors, ruined toys, lost masters

From the sirens

Beyond the scent of the hounds

Tao considers the bed beneath him. The pattern of black and white, the sharp-toothed zip. Hair shed from his body, now woven into the fabric as if part of the design. He was never comfortable in the bed, could never spend an entire night on its mealy support. He always sought out a better place.

Come

To a better place

The place you knew

The place you know

That thin film of hair over the calico and cotton.

It resembles a discarded skin.

Bring the boy here

Bring him home

Tao rises. He looks toward Woman and Man one last time. Boy's time in the bed has turned their heads. He sniffs. A faint trace of rot, hanging in the air like a cirriform cloud. Outside, spots of rain fall.

He exits the masters' bedroom with as much urgency as three legs can muster.

4

I paced in front of him like a caged animal. Tao, laying on the couch, watched my back-and-forth with eyes wide and ears primed.

"There's no other choice, Jay."

"There's always a choice."

"We need to leave. Before it's too late."

"You're overreacting."

"Am I? You think this state of emergency will end? You think things will return to normal?" I walked to the back door and stabbed a finger at the glass. "You think the Benitez family went on vacation?"

"Bess, come on. This isn't Nazi Germany."

"You sure about that?"

Jay shook his head. "Are you listening to yourself? You're sounding like one of them." He saw my look of horror and held up a hand. "Sorry. I didn't mean to suggest… I meant you're jumping at shadows. Seeing a plot on every corner. Look, we can't just get up and go. What about Gab? You want to uproot her? And Kasper? Jesus Christ, our boy!"

"You're not going to use our son as an excuse."

"He's not an excuse. He's a reason. He's the reason. We came here so he could have a better life. And now you want to leave because of a… a temporary phase?"

I slumped down into a chair. Sunken chest. Rounded shoulders. Too many punches to the solar plexus.

"This isn't a phase," I said. "This isn't temporary."

Tao searches. Pantry. Kitchen. The bench by the front door, cushion crusted with the residue of rice crackers. He noses into the entry closet where eight months ago, plunged into the first of many darknesses, Man's flashlight discovered Boy naked and shaking, covering his ears, powerless as the town grid.

No sign.

Tao sits, tongue hanging from his mouth, heart crash testing his ribs. He knows absconder energy. He met it once, toward the end of his short tenure in the training program. A large, thick male—much larger and much thicker than Boy—who sometimes roared like a bear but mostly squeaked like a mouse. Trainer attached him to the male and, in the first seconds of their connection, he felt it: a current fizzing through this foreign body. Every limb poised, every muscle ready.

Tao was uncomfortable in the role. He understood the instinct—he'd wanted to flee during his first fifteen months of existence, mostly when other dogs beckoned. For the male though, running wasn't a want. It was a need. And here he was, abruptly stopping and laying down at the slightest flinch, preventing this trapped animal, this leashed soul, from escape.

Boy has many needs: to sing, to jump, to shout, to laugh, to be sad when Girl is sad.

To run?

No.

He stays.

He doesn't leave without Family.

A noise. The familiar *rap-rap-rap* of small knuckles on thin wood. Tao hobble-dashes back upstairs.

*

The door is wide open. The hammock has been taken down and lies in a heap by the dresser. The desk lamp is turned off. Boy stares at the map of Gilder on the wall, eyes reduced to slits.

"Sudderly, the oven open…

"He jump out…

"Run through the door...

"Down the front paff..."

He runs a finger over the poster. Then he takes a step back, flicks his free hand. He tucks *The Gingerbread Man* under his arm and scans the floor. The black Sharpie is beneath a T-shirt with *LET IT BE* on its chest. He removes the cap, kneels before the small purple table and starts to draw.

A house.

Trees.

Lines. Up, down, across.

Two bumps.

A clover leaf.

A long tube.

A *T*.

A house with a plus sign.

*

Tao sits at Boy's hip. He watches. Waits. The worn red patches on his body whine and keen, pleading for the relief of a coarse tongue. He ignores them.

Seconds pass.

A minute.

He is tempted to bark. It might work. It might also alert the hounds. Bite? An abhorrent thought. He's never bitten anyone before, let alone Family. And even if such a disgrace were possible, would it have the desired effect? Boy would match the hurt with punches, slaps, maybe even his own bite. When the self-harm was complete, would Boy be capable of anything resembling obedience?

Tao swallows, then cranes forward, mouth open, teeth bared. He bites the corner of *The Gingerbread Man* and gently tugs. It doesn't budge from Boy's locked arms. Undaunted, the dog digs into the carpet with his front paws and pulls. Though the resistance is unwavering, the book wriggles and jerks, then slides free.

*

Kasper stops drawing. Still on his knees, he replaces the cap on the black Sharpie, drops it on the table then turns to face the thief. Tao stares back at him, fanned book hanging from the mouth like a giant moth. He frowns. Although the book is undamaged, it's jarring to see it in Tao's jaws.

Kasper feels heat in his throat, in his cheeks. He drags the headphones down to his neck. His voice shifts up an octave.

"Tao turn...

"Tao tuuuuurn...

"Sharing...

"Shaaaaaring...

"No play Tao...

"No play..."

*

Tao hop-steps back to the threshold of the room. He doesn't want to run—his injured leg, manageable when standing still and walking slow, could eat him alive in the chaos of a sprint. He will if needs must, though. Out of the room, down the stairs and out of the front door. Once outside, he would slow down again. Give the book back and start the long journey to safety. He senses Boy will follow once outside.

Another hop-step. A slight lift of the head. Tao's stomach rumbles and rolls, a troll beneath the bridge of his good intention. He could devour the book, tear into its glorious paper and ink. He can't remember the last food he ate—certainly it was before the arrival of the hounds. How long ago? Forever ago.

He watches for a sign: a nod of the head, a shuffle forward. Something to show that Boy understands: passage to a better place lies ahead, and loyalty to those lost is past.

*

Kasper clears his throat, taps his thigh. He turns back to his Sharpie art. With one eye closed, he grips the sides of the table and brings his face down to the purple surface. Moving back and forth, he takes a deep breath over each scribble. A full minute is needed to complete the task.

Kasper pivots to find Tao still in the doorway, three legs steady, book dangling. He lifts the headphones back onto his ears, pulls the brown blanket tighter around his shoulders.

He stands and shadows the dog out of the room.

*

The pair slowly descends the stairs. Although Tao senses the danger and the difficulty of the world between here and his former training site, he is, at this moment, happy. His skin is a millpond. His fractured leg, a distant storm. And Boy is at his heel. Submissive. Following.

The tether used with the absconder male—he wishes he had one for Boy, as prompt rather than prevention. He has seen Boy slow to move in urgent circumstances. One occasion, on a walk to the village, there was a construction site where a number of pylons had been knocked down. One by one Boy replaced them, each carefully positioned to restore a perfect perimeter. By the fourth cone, traffic was bearing down. Boy didn't care. Or cared too much. With horns blaring and rage being hurled from open windows, Man scooped Boy around the hips, lifted him off his feet, and carried him to the sidewalk.

Tao knows there won't be a tether on this voyage. And trickery such as stealing a book will wear thin, like the hair on his compromised skin. Ultimately, achieving safety will require the trust of Boy.

*

At the bottom of the stairs, the silence in the house is shattered by the wail of a siren. Pulses of yellow light flood the blinds. Clomping boots litter the pavement. Diesel and cordite choke the air. The damaged front door creaks open an inch then settles back to its original post.

Tao cowers, tail tucked between his legs. *The Gingerbread Man* falls from his mouth.

He looks behind.

*

Kasper stands on tiptoes, hands pressed against his headphones. When the siren cuts out, he runs a finger along the handrail. Then he lays down on the steps and shifts onto his side, face six inches from the wall. He whispers.

"Help...

"He iss getting away...

"They began to chase...

"Run, run...

"Fass as you can..."

*

White noise, swirling and crashing. Low voices. Loud voices. Feet running. *Pop-pop-pop-pop-pop*. Bodies toppling. Human shrieks that could substitute for the sirens. Tao stares at the splintered door that stands between madness and survival, between the long beginning and the swift end to his mission. Inevitably, it will be thrown open by the relentless, hunting hounds. A certain death? Not if they steal down the corridor, through the living room and out the back door. To escape, though, requires a first step.

He is frozen.

His broken leg is a contagion, infecting the other three. From the chest down, he is numbed to the point of dead weight.

The hounds pass by again, shadows darting like dragonflies. One slows, stops at the door. Tao can hear the breathing—deep, deliberate inhalations. Then the hoarse scrape of metal dragging across concrete. Tao smells body odour and tobacco. He senses joy borne by malevolence, a peach with maggots for a stone.

Boy still lies on his side, wrapped in his blanket, facing the wall. Unmoved. Unable to move. The contagion has spread. Boy is silent now, too. Sleeping, perhaps. Dreaming of a time that will sustain him beyond the darkness. Dreaming of Family.

Tao closes his eyes.

*

The jacket finds his body as it did before—threads descending, spreading over his coat, strengthening like a covalent bond. There is an extra piece to the tunic this time: a cord. Braided and golden, it winds across the carpet and up the stairs until it reaches the prostrate figure of Boy. It loops around the left wrist three times and tightens.

A tingling in Tao's chest. A spawning warmth. Embers in his lungs are flung to the furthest reaches of his body with each expelled breath. His legs are alive again. Even the fractured limb feels whole. He steps forward, off of the stairwell landing and onto the floor. He expects resistance, the cord taut and straining against Boy's slumped form. There is none. Another step. Another. The movement still unpunctuated. And he hears it now: the shift of weight, the shuffle of feet, the stretch to retrieve the book. The tap of a finger on plastic headphone casing and the huff of a blanket opened wide like unfolding wings. Tao looks behind a third time. Boy is in tow, eyes big and unblinking, oblivious to the tether; the golden rope anticipating every move, the wrist manacle shimmering in the sunlight.

The door remains still.

The shadow of the hound still stalks its crumbling borders.

They hustle along the short corridor. Cross the lake formed by Tao's overturned bowl. In the living room, the destruction sets a hitch in their stride. One corner of the rug burnt black. Television screen gouged. Two dozen or more books removed from the bookcase and destroyed, their monstered pages littering the sofa and the rug. On the walls, fat smears of white paint spell out a warning that is wasted on the two onlookers.

Arriving at the back exit, they find the sliding glass door open; so, too, the wooden gate leading out into the no man's land of green spaces and hemlock trees and the parade of townhouses that end at the sidewalk of Sixty-Eighth Street. The screen door, however, is shut flush to the frame, without a gap where a nose or a paw might find purchase.

Tao fronts Boy, panting. Turns his head toward the thin wall of grey mesh. Turns back to Boy. He has seen Boy open the screen many times, usually when commanded. The instances of opening without prior instruction coincided with Woman's absence. Boy would fling the door aside, march into the courtyard and pace along the fence line, repeating the same anxious mantra over and over and over again: "Mommy's gone away... Mommy's gone away... Mommy's gone away..." It didn't seem to matter that Woman always returned, or that she always returned through the front door, or that Man's reassurances of her return never failed to deliver on their promise.

Tao considers the golden cord. It rolls and waves like a grasping tentacle. He shifts to the wrist restraint. The cuff offers a glimmer, but not of hope. He knows a second connection—one that will command Boy to open the door—won't be supplied by the jacket. He leans against Boy's leg and whines. A grunt in reply is the only reward for his effort. He pushes again, with greater force. It prompts a quiet "shoosh" and a stop-hand thrust in his muzzle. He glances at the corridor. It has transformed into a jungle. Trees line the walls. The floor is bare earth. A lush canopy obscures the ceiling. What remains of the passage is dark, forbidding. The front door has disappeared.

There is urgency in Tao now. And a kernel of anger. He barks, a terse order summoned from the pit of his gut, a warning issued by an impatient superior. The room shudders. The television pitches forward and falls to the floor. Torn pages dance, then settle. As the echoes die away, Boy curls like an autumn leaf, shrinking in fear. Tao pivots and steps toward the screen.

Until he turns back around, he is blind to the true source of the dread.

*

The woman stands ten feet away. Short and boxy, she might have been a gymnast before answering the call to reclaim her country. Her brown uniform—storm-cloud grey to Tao's eyes—is muted beneath a black bulletproof vest. The tight strap securing her helmet burrows under her cleft chin. The holster at her left hip is empty. The gun it held is trained on Kasper.

"Drop the blanket and slowly take off the headphones."

Kasper stands on tiptoe, then jumps in the air.

"You hear what I said? Drop the blanket and slowly take off your headphones."

Kasper narrows his eyes to slits. He starts to laugh. Giggles, then snorts, then great whoops. Amidst the glee, there are breathless shouts.

"THEY BEGAN TO CHASE! RUN, RUN! FASS AS YOU CAN! OH DEAR ... OHHHHH DEAR ..."

The woman pulls her shoulders back. Adjusts her aim from chest to head. "No games, kid. I will shoot you good and dead."

"OHHHHH NO ... POOR FING ... WAAAAAHHH!"

"Guess I have to count to three ..."

"WAAAAAHHH!"

"One ..."

"ONE!"

"Two ..."

"TWO!"

"Three."

"ONE-TWO-THREE-FOUR-FIVE ... SIX-SEVEN-EIGHT-NINE-TEN ... ELEVEN-TWELVE!"

The woman lowers the gun and replaces it in the holster. "Okay, okay. I get it. You're a retard. I had to make sure."

She unclips the chinstrap, takes off her helmet, sets it on the table. A windsock of lime-green hair falls across the right side of her face and brushes her neck and collarbone. The left side of her head is shaved. It displays a biblical quote tattooed in cursive: *He will yet fill your mouth with laughter and your lips with shouts of joy. Job 8:21.*

"Can you talk proper? Can you answer questions?"

Kasper reaches down and grasps a page torn from one of the destroyed books. He holds it high, pincered between index finger and thumb. He lets it go. It twists and writhes in the air, then settles on the toe of his left sneaker.

"This your dog?" she asks. "Looks like someone fucked up his leg. It wasn't you, was it kid? If you say yes, I'm going to empty my clip into your face. Was it you? Don't say yes."

"Yes."

"I said don't say yes."

"Yes."

"You're just repeating the last thing I say, yes?"

"Yes."

The woman laughs. "Easiest confession I ever had." She gets down on her haunches, gaze fixed on Tao. "What's his name?"

"They run affer him. They wan to eat him."

"Some name." The woman snaps her fingers and pats the floor. "Come here, boy. Come on. I'm not one of those filthy Defs. Come."

*

A glance at Boy. Silent now. A good thing. Eyes, too, are still, trained on the floor. He senses their message. Opening the screen door is out of the question.

The hound is on her knees now, bending low, hands clapping. She continues to call him. The voice is not unkind; there is friendliness, perhaps even tenderness in its pitch. The smell of her skin is undeniably disturbing—a hideous riot of dark places visited and foul deeds done. The energy beneath the odour, though, is benign.

She won't hurt him.

She won't hurt Boy.

Tao licks his lips. He studies the cord. It has lengthened. The extra give has created two grapefruit-sized loops. The wrist manacle is more like a sleeve now, extending almost to the elbow. He feels the jacket's pull, compelling him to move closer.

Trainer speaks.

Go on, Tao

You know what to do

He takes a step away from the screen.

Toward the hound.

*

"That's a good boy," says the woman. "Keep coming." She nods at Kasper. "He knows a good guy when he sees one."

Kasper tucks his right hand into the waist of his jeans. He is no longer tracking with his peripheral vision. He stares directly at Tao.

"I'll take care of you," continues the woman. "Both of you."

*

Don't second-guess, Tao

There is no other way

Put some distance

Between you and the screen door

He steps again.

Head low. Eyes locked, unblinking.

The pull of the jacket remains steady.

"You're lucky I found you. Some of my buds out there—they don't draw the line at retards. Dogs, sure. But not retards."

Keep going

Don't stop

Not yet

Fifteen feet.

Twelve.

Ten.

Tao looks over the hound's shoulder to the hallway jungle. The passage has succumbed, the growth dense to the point of strangulation. It is a metastasizing tumour. The vines forming its irregular borders have reached the dining table and the piano tucked against the northern wall.

*

"My older sister Terri has a retarded girl. Grace-Marie. She's not the same as you, kid—she's got that spaz thing. Serial palsy, or whatever it's called. Terrible. She's always pretty happy, but it's hard. On her, on Terri... the whole family. It breaks your heart."

The woman airs a bitter laugh.

"Fucking Defs think they're hard done by. What a joke. They should go live with Terri and little Gracey-Marie for a few days."

She cocks her head to one side, listening to the strains of sirens farther south.

*

That's good, Tao

Far enough from the screen door

Close enough to her

Inches away from the hound's outstretched arm, her hand palm down in a gesture of peace. Tao stares at the fingers—short, thick, nails lined with dirt, knuckles red and angry.

He pictures them holding the gun again.

You're there

The hound's face. Instability in her features; a bubbling, as if her skin has come to a boil. Her blue eyes have turned black.

You're ready

Cheeks bunch. Furrows appear in the forehead. Lips peel back, exposing the teeth.

Her canines are oversized and sharp. Saliva drips from their lethal points.

Go

Tao turns and runs.

5

I stared, one eye half-closed.

"You want us to keep him."

The trainer patted Tao on the head. "It's up to you."

"There's nowhere else for him to go?"

"There's a wait-list of people who want a good companion."

"I mean, nowhere else he can be of service?"

She shook her head. "We're looking at a PTSD *support program for the ones who don't complete. But only if the Reparation Party doesn't win the election. They'll pull our funding."*

"It's kind of sad to see him without his jacket."

"Yeah, it is. A superhero who lost his powers."

I scratched my neck, nodded, then bent forward. The dog dipped his head and considered me with black-rimmed baleful eyes. He knows, I thought. He knows we're charting the course of his life.

We hadn't become a billet family in the hope of being gifted a pet. Until now, I hadn't even known it was a possibility. There were reasons to say no, to continue being a caretaker. Dogs that stayed with us and completed training—there'd been three prior to Tao—they left to go to work, to do good. The loss wasn't easy, but the dogs exited our lives healthy, happy and young. The same couldn't be said for a pet's goodbye.

"We have a son." After a pause, I added, "With challenges."

The trainer nodded, aware of the fact but unsure of what to say.

"There's a lot of stories, you know? About animals with kids like Kasper. How they help them. 'Unlock' is the word they use. Dog, cat, horse, hamster, turtle, whatever—it unlocks the child. Opens him up. Brings back the child the parents used to know. The child they mourned for. They see the animal as a saviour. Rescued the child from torment, from a fate worse than death." I looked skyward and scoffed. "Hallelujah, it's a miracle!"

I cupped Tao's muzzle in my hands. The dog met my gaze.

"You don't have to save our boy," I said. "He needs help, sure. He'll need it his whole life. But he doesn't need it from you. He doesn't need to be saved."

Tao expects retribution. Anger. Screaming. *Pop-pop*. Perhaps the crash of a fist on his back or those frightful jaws closing around his neck. He understands—the jacket will not protect him from the hound. It is there for the service of others, not for his benefit.

Piston breaths. Jackhammer heartbeats. He wonders if he'll reach the screen door. If he makes it, he hopes the cord connecting him to Boy is strong, the cuff secure.

The woman claps her hands. "Hey! Woah! Don't go! I'll take care of you!"

Tao launches himself at the screen. For a fleeting moment, it is a wall. Bricks and mortar and false promise. Then he is upon it, pouring through it. The door frame buckles like a staggered fighter. The thin wire mesh explodes in clouds of grey smoke. Walls crumble and windows heave. A blizzard of torn pages covers the tracks of his escape.

There is no sound. No shout. No *pop*.

Only breaths, beats.

He runs. Through the courtyard, out of the gate. A stormwater drain hisses. Hemlocks along the fence line nod and shake in the wind, torn between approval and admonishment. The ryegrass streams beneath his frantic paws. At the far end of his tunnel vision is a glimpse of Sixty-Eighth Street: downed power lines, a bin laying on its side, a black truck with smashed windows. Tao hopes to stop running when he reaches the sidewalk, but it's not up to him. The jacket is his master. It chooses the moment.

In the first strides beyond the boundary of the townhouse complex the choice is made. The force propelling him gives out. A scythe of pain from his broken leg shears through his chest and hips. Tao yelps and pitches forward. His right front paw catches a divot in the ground, slinging his lower body into the air. The world stretches and blurs. He flails through the rotation of his body, a clay target clipped, then crashes, nose and chin branding the sidewalk with a smear of blood.

His limp body comes to rest by a pair of young, straggly cedars. At their base is a litter of empty shell casings, bad seeds trying to take root in the patchy soil.

*

No movement on Sixty-Eighth Street. No speeding cars or defiant trucks or bloated vans stuffed with extended families and all their worldly possessions. No people running or stumbling or crouching low as they dart between the shadows. Houses are locked out of fear or left for the ghosts. A few are boarded up. In the sky, the clouds falter. On the ground, the trees dare not twitch. They await the next act of the main players: the conquering Homeland forces, the regrouping Defiance rebels. But the theatre has moved elsewhere.

From the top branch of a curbside cherry blossom, a blue jay jeers. Distant sirens answer the taunt.

*

Tao licks the dirt from his front left paw. Agony rules his body like a despot. He is unsure where one pain ends and the next begins; they've merged into a single tempest, each storm cell indistinguishable from the whole. He steels himself and lifts his head, turns slowly—every inch a trial—to view his wretched form. His ribs are stark and flecked with mud. His back rises and falls like overworked bellows. The broken limb is at a horrifying new angle—wrenched skyward, it appears more like a fledgling wing than a fractured leg.

Jacket—gone.

Cord and cuff—gone.

He turns back, drops his head between his front paws. A clutch of whines ekes out of his throat. In the company of thin cedars and spent bullets, he shuts his eyes, waits for the presence within, the voice of Trainer, to soothe him. You are good, Tao. You did what was asked of you. You did everything you could.

It doesn't come.

All he hears are echoes of Boy.

Help!

He iss getting away!

The dog whimpers. Lays flat on his side. He considers rolling over onto his back, soft belly exposed, but the effort required is too great.

They ran affer him

Shouting and screaming

A touch. A nudge to the shoulder. Could be a finger, or a stick. Maybe the barrel of a gun.

He stops whimpering. He expects the echoes of Boy to cease too, but they continue.

All free of them

Racing and chasing

And they are louder now. Clearer. No longer within. Around. All around. And close. By his ear.

These are not echoes. This is not memory's doing.

This is—

No moor sleep, Tao

Time to wake up

—the call of duty.

*

"Wake up, Taaaaaaooo.

"Wake-up-wake-up."

*

He opens his eyes, blinks away the dappled sunlight.

Boy is seated in front of him.

*

Kasper sits cross-legged, jeans rolled up to just below the knee. Sneakers to shins streaked with mud. Shirt sleeve torn. Face and neck the colour of rock salt. He draws deeply through his nose, the rhythm of his normal breathing pattern almost regained. A handful of raindrops dot his headphones like blisters. His narrowed eyes are fixed on the open book in his lap.

"Can't catch me," he says. "I'm the Ginnerbread Man."

*

Tao eases over onto his belly and tucks his good legs in and under his frame. On the third attempt, he manages to stand. Boy's eyes remain on the book. Tao leans forward, his chin nearly on the pages. His gurgling stomach—it's no distraction. He sniffs Boy's hand then gives the knuckles a lick. He expects the standard reaction, etched over five years—withdrawal, frowns, anxious laughter.

*

Kasper lifts his hand from the book, closes it into a fist. Examines his knuckles as if they were precious gems, turning them this way and that, bringing them to the tip of his nose. He nods and wipes them on the grass.

He rises then walks to the curb on tiptoe. Holding *The Gingerbread Man* in a double-arm wrap against his chest, he looks right, south, toward the city. The tall buildings' backdrop of snow-dusted mountain range is ringed with grey smog. Kasper looks left, north, toward the border. The land is bare, missing the fall pumpkin patches that were a staple for three generations. He drags his headphones down to his neck and frowns, considering the stranger that is Sixty-Eighth Street. Once upon a time it was a seat beside the educational assistant on the school bus, and walks with Mom to the 7-Eleven, and wide eyes at house 4805's holiday lights. It hasn't been that fairy tale for a while. He stares at the asphalt canvas before him. It is an abstract of skid marks and hurled bricks and broken glass.

Kasper steps into the street.

*

Boy has many needs: to sing, to jump, to shout, to laugh, to be sad when Girl is sad.

To run?

No.

He stays.

He doesn't leave without Family.

But what if Boy is forced to leave without Family? And there's no possibility of return?

Wouldn't he run?

Tao scrambles forward. His head throbs. White spots muddle his vision. Past the clouds in his eyes, he can see Boy in the middle of the street, looking left, looking right. The distance to cover is vast, but not unconquerable.

Tao stumbles at the curb. Falls. His damaged leg slaps the hard tarmac and, for a few seconds, the world burns. He opens his mouth wide, swamping his tongue with cool air. Then he regathers his essentials—limbs, breath, courage. An eon later, he is upright.

In the street, Boy hasn't moved.

*

Kasper stands on the white line, *The Gingerbread Man* tucked into the back of his jeans. A cool breeze darts along Sixty-Eighth. It ruffles the torn sleeve of his T-shirt, brings goosebumps to his forearms. Chills the tears in his eyes and on his cheeks. He wishes Mom was here. Dad and Gab. He wishes he had his blanket.

He looks only south now, toward the city and the mountains. He wipes his eyes, his nose. Behind him, is the scrape of Tao's nails on the asphalt. He nods three times.

"Spotted dog saw him...

"Win I catch you...

"I will gobble you up."

*

Tao closes in, lurching and listing, his movement more sea lion than dog. His gaze, though, is steady, focused on the closing gap. Boy is still within reach. But that could change in an instant. A quick jog, a skip. A march, feet stomping, arms swinging high—one of Boy's staples in moments of frustration or defiance. Any one of these and salvation may be lost.

It may be lost regardless. Danger looms—Tao feels it, a small searchlight peering through the sensory fog. The hound they encountered at the house would've summoned the pack by now. They'll be seeking. Before long, finding.

He edges closer.

Closer.

And there.

Tao latches onto the hem of Boy's jeans. With the meagre strength remaining in his injured lower body, he sets, then pulls. Boy doesn't budge. He pulls again, the second attempt weaker than the first. No give.

He holds, nose twitching as if pollen were in the air.

You hope the jacket returns, but it does not come for you

You wish to steal the book again, but it is out of reach

Stop hoping, wishing

You brought him through the screen door, away from the house, beyond the attack of the hound

Lead on

The dog releases his hold and sits by Boy's hip. After a short pause, he rises and limp-walks twenty metres down the street, headed north. He skirts the charred remnants of a stack of placards then steps over the hunched stick figure of a fallen streetlight. Near a trashed red suitcase, hacked open and emptied by thieves unknown, he stops and turns to face Boy. He sits again.

*

An orange flare arcs across the northern skyline. Kasper watches it burn, then twists his lips and scrunches his nose. He pivots. The dog stands opposite the white Willow Pointe sign, staring at him. Kasper puts his hands up over his eyes and peeks between his fingers. The heels of his sneakers rise and fall like ancient empires.

"Run, run…

"Fass as you can."

He lifts the headphones from his neck, slips them over his ears. Checks that *The Gingerbread Man* remains tucked into the back of his jeans. His gaze slides away from the dog and settles on the white line beneath his feet. He brings his left hand up in front of his mouth. With his right, he waves.

"Bye-bye, everybody.

"I love you.

"Byyye."

He takes three deep breaths then walks down the street. When he reaches Tao, he places his right hand above the dog's head, palm down. Runs it down the neck, along the spine. Touches the flickering tail with his index finger.

"And now, they join in chase."

*

The pair shift back to the sidewalk and make their way toward the dead traffic lights at the junction of Sixty-Eighth Street and the Trunk Road. The hobbled dog leads, never straying more than two body lengths ahead. The boy follows, silent but for the hand tapping his thigh.

*

Approaching noon. Sun at its highest rung.

Caravans of clouds obscure its view of the destruction below.

6

By the tepid glow of a Coleman lamp, I emptied a second bag of ice into the cooler. Tao sniffed a stray cube that slid across the floor and came to rest by the idle fridge.

"The Sheldricks sent their kids away. Put them on a train this morning."

I replaced the lid on the cooler then sat down, head buried in my hands. Quiet sobs, so as not to wake the rest of the house.

"I can't do that," I added, wincing at the pinprick of the words. "Just can't."

Tao moved close, rested his chin on my knee.

"Gab might make it, if she was on her own. With Kasper though ... "

I stood and grabbed a washcloth—the one I'd used throughout the day on the foreheads of my children—and blew my nose. I rinsed the washcloth in the sink. In the poor light, you couldn't see the water quality. I was grateful. A few streets over, a single Roman candle whistled and screamed and crackled then burned out. New Year's Eve. It didn't feel like a beginning or an end. It felt like the train I couldn't allow my kids to board. Leaving the station, rounding the bend. Disappearing.

"I would never tell this to anyone but you, pup."

The dog tilted his head. My small voice and grave tone was concerning. He wagged his tail, hoping to help my next words be bigger and brighter.

"Been having this dream the last few months. I'm in a clinic somewhere. Not here—somewhere overseas. Some country that hasn't lost the plot. I'm in a bed, hooked up to machines, wires coming and going every which way. I'm dying. Not sure from what, cancer maybe. I feel like my insides have been hollowed out and the only thing left is my heart. It's kind of punch-drunk, trying to do the job of all the missing organs. It'll give out before long.

"The doctor comes in—she looks like my grade four teacher, Ms. Baxter. Short, glasses. Bit of chin stubble. She speaks in a language that isn't English, but I understand every word: You are committed to this? Yes, I am. You don't want more time to think it over? No, I don't. You understand there is no turning back once we begin? Absolutely. The doctor nods and pulls the curtain aside on the neighbouring bed. Kasper is there."

I paused. A siren. In the vicinity of the Roman candle. I waited for it to cut out, then resumed.

"He's dressed in his pajamas, the ones with Sasquatch on them. Stuffed tiger tucked under his arm. The Gingerbread Man *on the bedside table. He looks over at me. The little crease in his brow—his way of saying 'Mama, where are we? Who is this person? Why are you in bed? Are you sick?.' It's okay, my love. Everything is okay. There's nothing to be afraid of. Not anymore. Hey, show me your happy face. He gives the thin-lipped grimace that never fails to make me smile.*

"Ms. Baxter moves toward him, syringe in hand. He's singing the pinball number song from Sesame Street *when she injects him. And then he's gone, pup. Just like that. Just like the words he had when he was two. Then Ms. Baxter is at my side, sliding the needle into my arm. As I start to fall asleep, I wonder if my beautiful boy has found those words again.*

"First time I woke from the dream, I was shaking, sweating, heart like a hamster in a wheel. Second time was awful too, but it didn't have the same effect. A little less again for number three. By the time I'd reached a dozen, it was actually tolerable. And once I'd got to twenty..."

I closed my eyes, brought a hand to my mouth. Let my head fall forward. I sensed Tao waiting for a command. Sorry, pup—nothing to say. I rose from the cooler, turned the lamp down and climbed the stairs.

No night light in Kasper's room—only the feeble wash of a glow-in-the-dark poster of the solar system. I knelt by his bed. He was in his usual sleeping position: on his right side, limbs at a variety of angles, brown blanket weaving over and under his thin frame like a python on a tree branch. I laid a hand on his back. Breathing. Skin warm to the touch. I sat in the beanbag by the small purple table and wept silently.

Minutes became hours. Sleep stalked the room, unable to find a foothold.

Tao remembers the way.

When he was in the program, Trainer transported him back and forth. In the mornings, she appeared at the front door, greeted him with a high squealy voice and bundled him into the back of the white van where Assistant and two, sometimes three other dogs were waiting. The ride to the facility was always the same—exciting and worrying and long enough for his bladder to fill. It was signposted with smells: gasoline and fried grease early on, fish and salt in the middle, fertilizer and hay toward the end. He didn't pine for the pack during the trip; Woman, Man, Girl and Boy were little more than caretakers at this time, keeping him warm and fed and comfortable on nights and weekends. Ties that bind would come when the rides ended.

Five years after the final drop-off, Tao is headed to the facility again. No Trainer, no van. No excitement. No Family to send him off. No Family to come home to. Just Boy and duty and fear and fate.

And the way.

He remembers the way.

*

Two hundred metres from the T-junction of the Trunk Road, they shift from the asphalt to the sidewalk. The dog feels better there. Trees, hedges, driveways. Chances to hide, routes for escape. In his bones he knows the keys to survival: never be cornered, always have an out. Even on the Crusoe's island of Sixty-Eighth Street.

Stay alert. Senses sharp. Tao glances at his crooked leg, bobbing around like an earflap. The damp grass is a balm for three prickling paws, but nothing can relieve the fourth. The only consolation in that fact? The constant bite will keep him on edge.

*

Tao is twice forced to stop before reaching the Trunk Road intersection. Both times it is due to Boy's distractedness.

The first incident takes place at an open manhole, its iron cover deposited into the front yard of the nearby house 4650. After easing around the hole, taking care not to slip, Tao watches Boy balk at following his lead. He barks once—a quiet but gruff rebuke. Boy ignores him and leans over the hole, staring into the black. Tao's tail drops. The confined space might be the lure. And maybe the darkness isn't so frightful now that home has been left behind.

Tao steps forward, stops. Boy stands tall. Scuttles over to the curb. Picks up three pieces of loose gravel, holds them in a closed fist against his forehead then returns to the manhole. One by one, the rocks are dropped in. When all three are gone, and the last *plunk* of the broken water surface is heard, Boy skirts the hole, ready to resume walking.

The second delay occurs at the bus shelter by the Odd Fellows Hall. Arriving, Tao drifts right and passes behind the shelter, taking advantage of the temporary cover. Coming out, he is alone. He waits—no sign. He wheels around to the front of the shelter, limping carefully through the debris. Boy is standing in the nook, staring at the only laminated glass panel that hasn't been reduced to stars. The dog looks around. No eyes watching. No feet approaching. Across the street, a sagging cable wire shivers through a wind gust. He sits beside Boy and stares at the panel.

A poster of the face. Old, pale. Lips thin and stretched. Teeth clenched. Eyes hard and black, like kidney stones. Tao saw the face many times at home on the TV. The energy of Family would shift when it appeared; relaxed became thorny, pleasant became cheerless. Woman and Man—their reactions were never comforting. They would shake their heads. Point, shout. Sometimes they argued. Always, the unhappiest one—usually Woman—made the face disappear, replaced by much friendlier humans laughing or eating or pressing their mouths against each other.

Tao turns his attention to Boy. He watches the movements. Head tilts left, right. Eyes widen, then narrow down to slits. Nose wrinkles. Mouth purses, as if sucking on a teat. Tao yawns and exhales. Is Boy performing for the face? He looks again at the panel. No, not the poster. Boy's own reflection in the glass.

Tao yawns again, disregards the needling itch in his left ear. He recalls Boy making faces at the bathroom mirror. If Man was accompanying him, there would be words to match. Happy, sad, angry, worried, proud. He understood: they were commands, it was training. The faces and the words—Boy needed to recognize them in himself and in others.

Now is not the time for training. Now is the time to lead. To serve. To move on.

The seventh face—a pinched frown with eyes all but closed—turns out to be the last. Boy glances at Tao, mimics the bark from the manhole delay, then exits the shelter. Fifty-one minutes after commencing their odyssey, they arrive at the Trunk Road intersection. They have travelled a quarter mile.

*

Puddles of grey water in the gouged sidewalk. A pyre of broken furniture at the gate of Douglas Manor, awaiting a lit match. And the smell of rot on the breeze. In the years before the lockdown, when freedom fanned its tail feathers and hate's wings were clipped, the Trunk Road bore the brunt of the fertilized fields in the spring and the recycling plant in the summer. This rot is new. Its season is fall.

They approach All Saints Church. The quote on the sign once read, *A new command I give you: love one another. As I have loved you, so you must love one another. John 13:34*. It is riddled with bullet holes, now as unreadable as the minds that considered it target practice. In the courtyard, the bronze statue of the Virgin Mary is splashed with white paint. Shattered stained-glass windows, eighty-two years into their depiction of the stations of the cross, decorate the car park like confetti.

*

Thirty metres down from All Saints, the Tannen Park Medical Centre has suffered a ramming attack. The back end of a red SUV juts out from the caved facade of the offices, as if the building has unhinged its jaw and is trying to swallow the vehicle whole. There are no bodies in the SUV or on the ground. No smoke. No blood. Any witnesses to the attack are long gone. The only token of life is the tall digital sign by the driveway to the centre's parking lot. Prior to the fighting, the sign alternated every five seconds between time and temperature. Now, the sign flashes the same time over and over:

5:05

5:05

5:05

*

At the corner of Sixty-Sixth, Tao pauses, ears cocked. A noise behind them. He tilts his head, shifts from the concrete path to the grass and resumes his limp-walk. Twenty metres farther along, he hears it again. Clearer this time. A metallic rattle. Padding feet. Some distance away but in tow, following their laboured progress. He looks to the side of Boy, expecting a glimpse of the source. No sign. Just ruins already forgotten.

Tao blinks, the hackles rising on the back of his neck. He's heard the sound before. The complete memory is a hair away from retrieval when a second noise overtakes the first. It comes from the grey coach house set back from the road; a raspy, heated fuss tumbling out of an open window on the second floor, carrying across the vacant block where Christmas trees were once sold.

*

Kasper presses his palms against the headphones. Not enough—the baby's cry can still be heard. The distress is incomparable to the devastations wreaked upon him by Gabrielle's tears, but it can't be ignored. He yanks the headphones down and jams a finger in each ear, pushing almost to the line of the first knuckle.

"Awww... so sad... so so sad...

"Baby's crying... Baby's upset...

"Don' cry... It's okay...

"It's okaaaaay..."

Knees bend, bend, until he is in a squat. The wails chisel at the cracks his index fingers can't fill.

*

Tao licks his lips. Boy's small voice will soon be loud, ten times the volume of the bawling child. He hobbles around to position himself behind the squat. The book clings to Boy's beltline. There for the taking.

He edges forward.

"It's okay, baby...

"Don' cry...

"It's okaaaaay...

"YES!"

He flinches at Boy's sudden shout, then looks around. The Trunk Road is still theirs. The follower with the metallic rattle and padding feet is silent, hidden. He pants and scooches in. *The Gingerbread Man* sits six inches from his muzzle. Saliva gathers in his mouth. He absorbs details: tiny dots of spattered mud on the front cover, the shiny circle in the top right corner, the tooth indentations left behind in the last heist.

*

A fracturing of the baby's cry. Coughing, choking, pocked with desperate wheezes. The struggle lasts for nearly thirty seconds. Then all is quiet, save the creak of the unfastened gate fronting the vacant lot.

*

Slowly, Kasper rises. At full height, he removes the fingers from his ears. No sound. He watches the grey coach house for a time, eyeing it as if it were haunted. Then he reaches behind and lifts *The Gingerbread Man* from his jeans. Through squinted eyes, he looks at the book, at panting Tao, again at the book. He drums his fingers on the cover then opens to a page. He reads aloud as he starts to walk:

"If I catch you...

"I will gobble you up!"

*

At the intersection of Liddon Avenue, they encounter a hearse from the nearby funeral home sitting half on the street, half on the sidewalk. The rear door is open and a casket angles down, foot first, onto the asphalt.

The lid is raised.

At first glance, the body is waxen and smooth, on the verge of turning. Closer inspection reveals it is not flesh and bone but plastic, a mannequin stolen from one of the clothing shops in nearby Durant Park Square. It is naked. It wears a white blindfold. Where its mouth once was is a hole the size of a tennis ball, blasted by a Remington 870 from close range.

*

In the world beyond Tao's comprehension, a beautiful tomorrow was gunned down. One minute it was soaring, climbing ever higher into the sky, prompting the grounded to gaze in wonder; the next it was plummeting to earth, mortally wounded by the commander-in-chief, a hunter seeking nothing more than the prize.

There was still hope: killing didn't amount to owning. Without possession, the hunter had nothing to show for his act of destruction. He had fired from a great distance—maybe his trophy had fallen into thick forest or deep water? Maybe it was out of reach? And if unclaimed, some other beautiful tomorrow would take its place and rise again.

But the hunter had retrievers. Thousands of them. Millions. Many felt unsure of their actions, uncomfortable doing the hunter's bidding. Some admitted to shame. But they couldn't defy their breeding, their essential nature. To do so required a breath of courage they were not willing to inhale.

Tao, though, is trying to breathe. And in spurning his instinct he doesn't ask for much in return, just something familiar and comforting he can carry in his mouth. One of his toys: the ring or the duck, the red bone or the blue shark.

He wishes he had one of them now—he would feel more like himself.

*

The approach to the service station on the corner of Sixty-Fifth Street is punctuated by the smell of cooked meat. Tao's stomach awakens, sloshing and juddering. Drool gathers in the corners of his mouth. At some point in the journey, he has to eat. Boy, too. Should it be here? Now? Tao stops by the price sign and licks his lips. He looks up at the sky. The clouds are thicker, darker. Rain may be on the way. He turns to his follower. A rare occurrence—Boy is staring directly at him, no humming or whispering, no fidgeting hands, feet flat on the ground.

Tao dips his head then pivots right, limp-walking toward the convenience shop and its octet of sentinel pumps.

*

The shop is a husk. Pictures and posters torn down. Shelves stripped. Cash register gone. Counter reduced to rubble. In the western corner, an empty fridge lays on its side, wading in a half inch of water. The light dangling from the cork ceiling stutters and flickers, Morse code messages saying nothing and going nowhere. A still-standing banner by the wrecked counter proclaims that the lottery jackpot of eighty million dollars could land you in a whole new world. A charred flag is pinned to the back wall, its centre symbol drowned in white paint.

Tao hop-steps along the thin aisles, laps the fridge water, sniffs the tile floor and the bare shelves. The meat smell is strong but diffuse, without a point of origin. It mingles with the service station staples: gasoline, grease, rubber. And a fourth unusual odour, acrid and bitter, infecting the lip of the fug. He drifts into the corridor where the washrooms are located. All the doors are shut. Four bullet holes pepper the Men's nameplate. Returning to the shop floor, he sniffs the square patch of dirt and dust that marks where the ATM once stood. Then he paws at the rug bunched against the razed cabinetry of the front counter. There is no food here, yet the aroma of cooked flesh is undeniable. Tao's guts yearn. Long drips of drool hang from his jowls.

He cranes his neck to get a better view of the shop's southern wall. There's an exit leading to the garage. The door has been knocked down; laying on the concrete it resembles the hatch of a basement cellar.

Boy stands at the threshold, nose pinched between forefinger and thumb.

*

The body is under a tarpaulin, next to the front left wheel of the sole vehicle in the shop: a school minibus. Five feet away stands a rusted turpentine can, lid removed, empty save a few drops. A blackened forearm and hand have escaped the plastic sheet. The fourth finger sports a gold ring, reminiscent of a Montecristo and its band.

Tao stares at the torched limb, his mouth dry, stomach a white-knuckled fist. He hunches and shits, thin brown gruel pouring from his anus like cola from a can. The painful surge lasts a few seconds, then subsides. He lurches away from the mess and scrambles back to the shop side of the school bus. Though his senses reel, his mind is on a fixed point: it was a mistake to come here. A terrible mistake. They must leave, before the smell takes hold of him again, before his insides make him come completely undone.

Boy remains at the garage's entrance, disengaged from the body, the shit, the urgency, the mistake.

*

A red button on the wall. Kasper stares at it close up, one eye shut. He presses it quickly as if it is hot to the touch. No noise. No motion. He presses again, hand lingering this time. Still no response. Frustration sets in: small whines and flicks of the fingers. A jump on the spot. He hits the button with the butt of his hand. Again. And again. A pair of flies buzz around the commotion. Defeated, Kasper pats his headphones and squeezes into a small corner gap between the workbench and the garage door frame.

*

Tao swallows, trying to loosen his throat enough to bark. But the time for admonishing Boy has passed.

A vehicle approaches, its rumbling engine like a seismic tremor.

*

Plain. No yellow lights. No sirens. The truck mounts the curb, clips a rogue tire lying in the driveway of the gas station and skids to a stop by an aged Jeep on concrete blocks. Two figures alight: a man from the cab, a woman from the cargo bed. The man is a medicine ball, round and leathery. Atop his bearded face and mirror-shaded eyes is a batting helmet dented above the earflap and stained with pine tar. A cigarette hangs from his mouth. Despite an absence of shoes, the woman is taller than her companion. She's thin, angular. Runnels of blood-red hair course down her back and shoulders. Both man and woman have guns tucked into their pants and wear brown uniforms, homemade. Several of the white felt letters on the back of their shirts have fallen off.

The man collects a thin length of hose from the bed and discards the cigarette, crushing it beneath his jackboot. He unscrews the Jeep's gas cap and inserts one end of the hose into the tank. Stretching the hose, he sucks on the open end of the tube, the exertion darkening the impact craters and lava flows of his moon face. After a full minute of futile effort, he spits out the tube and breathes deep. He gestures for the woman to come closer, to stand face to face. She complies, head bowed. He slaps her and hitches a thumb toward the garage. The woman, hand pressed to her struck cheek, shakes her head.

*

Tao tucks in behind the bumper and front right fender of the school bus, watching the scene. These hounds are matted and scruffy. Strays. Still dangerous, though. He senses the reek of their breath, the curdle in their blood.

Escape. No sneaking out of the garage door. The side exit? He and Boy would be less exposed in the shop, but the move could sink them. A sudden shout, a distracted wander, a rhythm tapped out on the thigh. Any one of the myriad ways Boy attracts attention and the strays will come running. Best to stay put, wait until they leave. Tao leans against the bumper. The smell of the burnt body burrows deeper into his skin.

He watches Boy standing in the corner. Body still. Mouth closed. Feet flat on the ground. Squinted eyes roaming the walls. Book held to the chest.

No inkling of peril.

*

On the wall above the garage's workbench are a few items neglected by looters. Kasper leans in close, head turned, examining each item from the periphery of his left eye. He squeezes the handles of a red jumper cable, opening and closing its jaws on his wrists. He pokes the small pile of greasy rags. He briefly tries on a pair of cracked safety glasses.

Then he settles back onto his heels. Looks up at the ceiling, down at the floor. From his mouth come tiny *chet-chet* sounds, as if a cricket has found a home beneath his tongue. He exhales, frowns. He eases *The Gingerbread Man* away from his chest and opens to a dog-eared page.

*

Trainer whispering in Tao's ear:

Book open

Finger down

Eyes following the words

You believe those words will be spoken soon

Announced

Tao summons a low growl then glances at the strays outside. They're arguing. Loud voices, pacing feet. No sign they heard.

*

Kasper looks up from the hardcover. He lifts his index finger from the page. For a few seconds, it arrests him: the chewed nail, the scraped knuckle, the whorls of the fingerprint.

*

He trusts you
But you do not trust him
In your eyes, he is not worthy
Too confusing
Too unpredictable

Tao growls again, crouching beneath the bus fender. The stark warning delivered: Close the book and keep quiet, Boy.

*

Kasper stops staring at his finger and brings it to his lips. He nods, taps the side of his headphones and resumes reading.

*

Without trust
The best you can achieve is
Obedience

Deep in Tao's gut sits a desire for Boy to be silent. Not just in the present, but for all time; from this moment until the last, whether the last be inside this garage or out on the street or near the marshlands or among the green bean farms or at the refuge of the training facility.

Why does Boy speak at all? What purpose does it serve? From day one, the utterances were clouds, aimless, insubstantial, always changing form. Over the years, they grew a little and acquired a modicum of shape. Tao came to recognize some: yes, no, wait, stop, good, bad. The vast majority, though, continued to puzzle. And not just him—Family, too. Countless times in the echoes of the noise, Tao saw their lost faces and sniffed their cowed scents. Even Girl—Boy's self-appointed translator—shrugged far more often than she nodded.

Boy, silent for good—it is an agreeable thought, but nothing more. Pointless words will still be said. Strange sounds will continue to be aired. And at some critical juncture, they must surely bring about their downfall.

Not this moment, though. The alarm is already tripped.

The strays have ceased arguing. The female is shuffling toward the open garage door.

*

Kasper closes *The Gingerbread Man* and holds it once more against his chest. He pulls his headphones down onto his neck. He watches Tao stare ahead, baring his teeth.

*

No training for this
Just instinct
Powerful, pure
Defend, protect
Fight

Tao waits for the first thread to descend, for the first touch on his back. What will the jacket bring this time? Whatever the new miracle, it must happen now.

The stray pauses a few strides shy of the garage threshold. She pivots and starts shouting at her partner, waving her arms.

Come, jacket.

Come.

*

"Come."

Startled, Tao wheels toward the source of the whispered command. A small door, no wider than a turnstile, has opened in the back wall of the garage. Filling out the bottom half of the space is a crouching man. His aging boots are tied with fishing line. The holes in the knees of his pants resemble the work of burrowing mice. A ragged raincoat—its red colour sun-bleached to a dull pink—is zipped up to his neck. Partially obscured by a mask, his face is creased and deeply tanned.

Clamped to each of the man's ears is a four-inch cone made from fruit-box cardboard, thin end inserted into the canal. A strand of rusty wire circles the midsection of each cone and wraps over the ear, keeping the cone securely in place.

"This way."

Tao looks over his shoulder—the female stray is sitting on the pavement now, arms folded. He turns back to face the rear wall. The masked stranger is still there, down low in the small doorway, cupping one of the strange cones on his ears, smelling of sweat and mud and blackberries. Not a trick. Not a dream. Not the work of a jacket miracle.

Tao glances at Boy. No change. Book pinned to the chest, headphones hanging from the neck.

Mouth shut.

The stranger's hand extends. Palm down, fingers curled under. The nail on the thumb is missing, skin on the third and fourth knuckles cracked.

Tao moves forward, each limp-step tamping down the sensory noise of turpentine and burnt flesh and shit. He sniffs. The stranger's hand straightens, rises, settles on Tao's head. A small squeeze is followed by a scratch behind his ear.

"Go get your pal."

Without trust

The best you can achieve is

Obedience

Tao inches out from the cover of the bus. The sight in the driveway doubles the staccato beat of his heart. The male stray is now in the frame. He stands over the female, hands in pockets, voice quiet and low, the first thunder of an imminent storm. He is at ninety degrees to the open garage door. A look to the left—even a momentary glance—would reveal an injured dog witnessing his actions.

Tao lurches forward, eyes fixed on the strays. The clicks of his nails on the hard floor are like cymbal crashes in his ears. As he nears Boy's nook, the driveway scene slides by, then disappears. Tao lowers his head. His muscles ease their frenzied grip on his bones. He exhales, a seam of tension unpicked with the expelled breath. For the moment, the strays cannot see him. First goal accomplished. The simplest goal.

He stares at Boy.

*

Kasper gets to his feet. He places *The Gingerbread Man* on the workbench, then stretches, arms above his head, hands interlocked. He lifts his headphones back up over his ears then retrieves the book and tucks it into the back of his jeans.

On tiptoe, Tao by his side, he takes three steps forward into the open before a scream stops him in his tracks.

*

A look once more to the driveway. The strays face out toward the Trunk Road. The female shrieks and claws, a handful of her red hair in the right fist of the male. Twice he attempts to drag her toward the open garage.

She starts to cry.

Tao turns to Boy, knowing what he'll find: the descent begun. Knitted brow, quivering bottom lip. Knees bending slowly like a tree branch laden with December snow. Body yearning for the ground. Tao scrambles into position, poised for Boy's total surrender. Is there any alternative to stealing the book? Perhaps the stranger intervening? Lifting Boy up, a hoist over the shoulder, a steal away from the danger? Boy wouldn't go quietly—the stranger isn't Woman or Man. He isn't Family. Without true comprehension of the imminent danger, Boy would view him as nothing more than a puzzling threat.

Mouth open, hackles erect, Tao hangs upon the inevitable.

*

Kasper, down on one knee, takes a deep breath. Another. A third. He lifts *The Gingerbread Man* from his jeans and presses it against his cheek. Then he thrusts the book toward Tao.

"Take," he murmurs. "Take."

*

Tao blinks, unsure of his response. He glances at the strays. The male is bent over, left hand in his pocket, right hand patting the gun at his hip.

The female is flat on the ground, legs and arms spread. He returns to the sidelong stare of Boy. Inches from his muzzle, the offer remains.

He takes the book in his jaws.

As he limp-dashes for the back of the garage, skirting the puddle of shit and the shrouded corpse, he can tell Boy is following by the low hum that trails him like a comet's tail.

*

Dog, boy and stranger emerge into the tepid sunlight. The stranger collects a double stroller parked by the exit. It is bloated with a variety of goods—canned food, bottled water, garbage bags, blankets, a radio. As the trio hustles toward the sidewalk that rings the closed Lighthouse Shopping Centre, Tao recognizes the sounds that stalked him and Boy on the Trunk Road: padding feet, metallic rattle. He seeks confirmation, knowing there will be none. Boy has eyes only for the book wedged in Tao's mouth.

Nearing the looted dollar store, a single gunshot echoes above the gas station. The trio breaks stride, waiting for the next sound. A clatter, a wail, an engine starting. Only silence. They trudge on, compass pointing northeast.

7

I sat on the bench, digesting the information. It didn't sit well. My stomach churned. I felt sure that any effort to stand up or shift in my seat or breathe deep would cause me to puke. So I sat still, back straight, while the words of the assessors poisoned my system.

"You need to know from the beginning: this is not good… He can't do these tasks… It's pretty obvious he is intellectually impaired… For the rest of his life, he will be dependent on others."

I watched Jay walk over from the playground and sit beside me on the bench. He smiled—lips as thin as rice paper—and laid a hand on my thigh.

"Look at our boy there," he said, pointing with the arm of his sunglasses. "You see that? See how he doesn't just barge through others to go first? He waits. He watches and he waits. If there's a smaller kid wanting a turn—he lets them go first. You see it, don't you? He notices. He understands."

His voice cracked on the final syllable. I felt the tension in his fingers.

"Fuck them," he continued. "They saw him for five minutes. Five goddamned minutes. And they've got Kasper all worked out, got his ceiling all sorted. Fuck them." He pivoted, lifting his right knee onto the bench. He took hold of my limp hand and kissed it. "They haven't got a clue, Bess. Nobody does. Not even us. I mean, we get that he's different in the way he feels and thinks. But maybe he knows *differently too. You know what I'm saying?"*

I shrugged.

"Clueless," he added. "They don't get to tell our boy's story. None of us do. Only him."

On the playground, our boy adjusted the tic-tac-toe blocks. A centre O *surrounded on all sides by* Xs.

"I didn't like the look of those two back there. Not one bit. Don't want to think what might've happened if they found you. The proper Homers—they have orders, targets; the ones pretendin' are just wild. They got the green light from on high. Yeah, lucky I was followin' you two. Did you know I was followin' a while? I think, pooch, you knew, yeah? On the Trunk, up by the funeral home. I think you caught me. Like a chaplain in a whorehouse, you caught me. Ah, well. Not as quiet as I used to be. Not since my hearin' went bad. I was quiet in Squad. The gunfire'd break out an' I'd be a mouse. Wouldn't shout, wouldn't scream. Just keep my mouth shut. Tread light. An' 'cause of that, I'd sort of blend in. Disappear. That's how I survived, yeah? That's how I made it home. See, people think you get killed 'cause they seen you. Nuh-uh. You get killed 'cause they *heard* you."

*

The stranger talks a lot. He started soon after they were out of sight of the gas station and hasn't stopped since. His voice is quiet though, muffled by the mask. And assured. The route—it's in the direction they're headed. Not so far off course that escape is required.

Tao couldn't if he wanted to.

He considers his position in the stroller: on his side, curled tight, strapped into the spare of the two seats. His busted leg hangs down toward the ground. Although every major shift and bump of the wheels fires a small arrow into the hide of the injured limb, he is grateful to be relieved of the dead weight.

"How you doin', pooch? Nice bein' carted along, yeah? You're a regular king of France on his throne. We got to that footbridge over Magee Creek an' I looked at your sad face an' your low tail an' I thought to myself, you need a hug. An' I gave you one 'cause I like hugs an' 'cause, yeah, I didn't think our young friend here was inclined. I think he likes readin' more than hugs. An' then I took a closer look at that messed-up leg, an' even though it wasn't as bad as a lot of the shit I seen in Squad, I thought to myself, pooch could do with gettin' off that messed-up leg. An' you look a lot happier now so I think I was right."

Tao turns, takes in Boy walking alongside the stroller. Hint of a smile. The odd skip in his step.

Happy to have his book back.

"A hunree crow in the sky want to take a bite."

"Ah, my young friend—you can talk! Wasn't sure up to now. Thought you might've been one of those silent types. No words, no voice. Only way to be in these here times, yeah. Or maybe I just wasn't hearin' you on account of the damage to my lugholes. So, was that a line from your book you said? I got a book, too. Got it here. *Chronicle of a Death Foretold.* Márquez. Been with me from day one. Know where I found it? A book burnin'! I kid you not. Came across a pile of ash far side of the village an' somehow this little beaut escaped the flames. Figured that was a good enough reason to keep it."

"I will get you ... I will munch you up, yum yum ..."

"I read it an' I thought it was the best story ever writ down on the page. I mean, I couldn't take my eyes off it once I started, yeah. It picked me up an' carried me away. It was ... magical. Guess that's why it didn't burn in the fire."

"Old man, old woman ... Little boy and the dog ..."

"Every time I read it—an it's got to be at least twenty times now—I always think the main guy's gonna make it, he's not gonna die. An' every time, I'm surprised an' sad when he dies, yeah. Which is ridiculous 'cause it's right there in the title—no escapin' it. I think it probably has somethin' to do with the writin'. An' the magic. Or maybe they're one an' the same."

*

They wander savaged back streets. At the junction of Tebbut and Washburn, the boy ends the exchange with unflinching silence. The man shrugs and flips the novel back into the tray beneath the stroller's seats. He asks the dog to ask the boy if he cares to do likewise with *The Gingerbread Man.* Tao pants in reply.

They lumber past hacked cedar hedges and marked front doors. Yard upon yard torched black, burnt offerings to the God of War. Crosswalks soiled with patches of dried blood awaiting the downpour that will return their stripes to white. Approaching the empty library—site of public protests before an anthrax scare shut the doors—they hear sirens. Not close, toward the eastern edge of town where the rail line streams toward the border. The dog whines. The boy stops and pulls the headphones away from his ears. The man lifts his face to the sky. A bald eagle overhead performs languid figure eights on the slow breeze.

"Sign of good luck, yeah," he says, pointing. "About the only thing they don't shoot."

Wounded dog, disabled boy, outcast man: to onlookers tracking their passage—survivors in the ruins praying for rescue, rebels needing allies to rise again—they are dashed hope. This trio can do nothing for them. And, in turn, nothing can be done for this trio. The briefest glimpse reveals they are not long for this terrible world.

*

"In the first weeks," the stranger says, speaking more to the trashed asphalt than the dog or the boy, "people saw me an' said, 'Why are you still alive? You're easy meat. You should've been the first to go.' They didn't understand: I was prepared. I'd seen this comin', yeah. From a mile away. Started with little things. Graffiti. Bad words. White paint. Then it was people losin' it in public. Neighbours turnin' on each other. Marches endin' up as riots. Folks getting outta town or just disappearin'. An' all the while, that fucker in charge is just fannin' the flames. By the time the Homers came along, the job was half done.

"I stocked up. Food, water. A few tools. I got this here radio an' a good battery. Then I kept my head down. Didn't give 'em a reason. They got plenty of those already." He lifts the mask and scratches the chin beneath his matted beard. "I did what I had to do to survive. Always done that. No different now."

*

On Westphail Avenue, outside a house peeled down to its studs, he stops. He notes the stares of both dog and boy.

"We're okay," he says. "Checked the airwaves last night. Homers went through here again a few days ago, yeah. Cleaned up the holdouts. Still gotta watch for the pretenders, though."

He walks forward to the mailbox. Aside from a lean in the post, it has survived the carnage delivered to the street. He opens the latch and looks inside. Empty, save for a wolf spider tending to the loose outer threads of its web. He closes the latch.

"Mr. Deng lived here. Split from his wife. Had his three kids every second week—older boy, two younger girls. If I remember correct, one of the girls was pretty good at gymnastics, before the gymnastics club became a shelter, of course. Yeah. He was a good man, Mr. Deng—a whole lot better than yours truly. Kept to himself. Never caused any trouble. An' he was so very good to me. He worked at the bakery, the little local up on Bontemps Lane. Whenever I'd come to the shop, he'd never kick me out like a lot of other places did. He'd let me try some of the samples. Sneak some of the older bread an' rolls to me out the back. Then one day he writes down his address on a paper bag an' tells me to come by his house in the afternoon an' check out the mailbox. I did what he asked because I knew Mr. Deng was a good guy. But I didn't know just how good until I got to the mailbox. I opened it up an inside were two beautiful pastries wrapped in plastic. An' five dollars. An' a little note, 'Same time next week.' Same time next week lasted three years."

He heaves the mailbox back into an upright position, then spits on the cracked driveway. Tao is otherwise occupied now, gnawing the red patch on his front left paw. Kasper continues to watch, but peripherally and through squinted eyes.

"When I found out Mr. Deng had been taken away, I knew it was someone on his street who'd called the Homers. Not sure who. But it doesn't matter now, yeah. Whoever it was, they got called out too. Everyone got called out in the end."

*

"Not far now. Just a couple of blocks."

The man steers the stroller beside the boy and his loping stride. They walk shoulder to shoulder. Squat shadows cling to their heels like desperate children.

"Nice headphones you got there, young friend. Bit better quality than my homemade hearin' aids. I like that we're opposites, yeah. You tryin' to keep the world out, me tryin' to let it back in."

Kasper shifts his headphones down to his neck, tilts his head to one side, fans the fingers of his right hand.

"You need to take a piss? I notice you been hangin' on to yourself. You prefer a toilet to the great outdoors? We can try an' find one before we get there if you're desperate to go."

Kasper tucks *The Gingerbread Man* into the back of his jeans. With each step, he scans the sidewalk for fallen leaves he can crunch underfoot.

"I know you can quote from that fine book of yours, but I suspect you don't have enough words for a proper conversation. Have I got that right?"

"Oh, dear! Oh, dear!"

"Okay. It's okay. Can you tell me your name?"

"Your name."

"Your name. You know? My name is ..."

"My name is ..."

"Is?"

"Is ..."

The man extends an open hand to the dog in the stroller. "Any advice, pooch?" Tao burrows down between his back legs and licks his crotch. "Helpful, yeah. Young friend, my name is Drew. And your name is ... Greg? Jeff? Doug?"

"Kasper."

"Cats purr?"

"Kassssss ... per."

"Ah, Kasper. Like the ghost, yeah?"

"Kasper."

"Okay, Kasper. Nice to meet you. An' how old are you? I'm guessin' fifteen, maybe?"

"Fifteen."

"An' what's your dog's name?"

"Dog."

"Prevents any confusion."

"Taodog."

"Pardon?"

"Taodog."

"Tay-oh, yeah?"

"Tay-oh ... yessss."

"*T-A-O?*"

"Yessss."

The man reaches around the side of the stroller and pats the dog on his bony head. "Okay, Kasper, Tao. You got a family? You tryin' to find 'em?"

Kasper stops. Frowns. Rubs his eyes.

"You tryin' to find Mom, Dad?"

"Ohhh, nooo!"

"No?"

"Aw, sad. So so sad!"

"Ah. I'm gonna assume Mom an' Dad aren't in the picture, yeah."

"Gab."

"Gab?"

"Gabbysister."

"Okay. Sister, too."

"So so sad. Waaaaaah."

"Can you tell me where you're goin', Kasper?"

"Run, run ... fass as you can."

"Right, this is a real stab in the dark ... Do you know the Defs? If you're tryin' to find them ... I'm looking for them, too. The Defs—you know where they are?"

"Can't catch me ... I'm the Ginnerbread Man."

The man looks at Tao and shrugs. "Worth a shot."

*

They arrive at a bungalow. Out front, the kidney-shaped garden has been trampled into mud. Punched through the roof is a hole the size of a wading pool. The front door hangs from the jamb like a half-severed ear, the lower hinge clinging onto the stressed screws for dear life.

"Stay here an' be a good boy, Tao," says the man. "I'll be right back." He turns to the boy. "There's probably a toilet in there. Doubt it'll be workin' but you may as well go an' have a look, yeah."

Hand on his groin, shifting from foot to foot, Kasper walks toward the gaping entrance. The stranger follows. Within seconds, both are inside, out of sight of the dog.

*

Tao's gaze darts from target to target. The doorway. The broken windows. The patch of gravel at the fence. The concrete path down the side. No glimpse of movement. He whines and strains against the seat belt keeping him in place.

He doesn't care for this destination. The smell, the energy—he senses this was a site of pain and misery. Not just in recent times; stretching back beyond the days when the world first began to unravel. He doesn't like that he can't see Boy. Woman and Man never lost sight of Boy, particularly around strangers. Though this human has behaved as a friend, he is still an unknown. And now he has brought them here, to a territory marked by disease and fear and confusion. For what purpose? To what end?

Tao examines his restraint then takes one of the straps in his mouth. The material is thin but dense, smooth on his tongue. The taste is sour, unappetizing. His stomach doesn't care—it roils like a rip current. He is beginning to chew when the stranger appears at the entrance and walks toward the stroller.

Tao's gnawing shifts, from between his teeth to down in his guts.

*

Once during training Tao was placed in the company of five damaged dogs. He understood his task: be calm, stay balanced, show them how to behave. What became apparent mingling with these fractured souls was that he could intuit much more than his role. The source of their suffering, the content of their abuse—he could connect with it as if it were his own. The sounds, the smells. The sights. An angry face shouting threats. A collar seized by a white-knuckled fist. And the weapon. A hard and rough stick. Not one for fetching. Lifted high like the biggest prize of the litter. Brought down with the force of a thunderclap.

Tao sees the weapon clutched in the stranger's right hand, looming larger with each step. It seems misplaced—the approach is calm, unhurried. No sign of anger. A smile behind the mask. And, yet, its presence is undeniable. Tao writhes in the seat. Without a solid purchase, the effort is wasted. He strains against the strap—it holds firm. He curls, tight as the belt will allow. Any hope of the jacket's return has gone. He wonders if it ever actually existed, if it was nothing more than a trick of the mind.

He barks.

You are the rescuer now, Boy. Help me. Please.

As I have helped you.

*

Kasper emerges from the building, jeans at his knees. He lifts them, zips up, fastens the button. *The Gingerbread Man*—secured under his arm while attending to his jeans—is returned to its back tuck. He half walks, half skips toward the stroller. He notes that the man is standing over Tao. In the man's hand is an object he's never seen before.

"Kasper. Perfect timin', yeah. I'm gonna need you."

*

Tao watches Boy settle in beside the stranger. Close enough to the stroller. Within reach of the restraint.

Free me, Boy.

You see the weapon. You know what it's for.

Free me.

*

Through squinted eyes, Kasper continues to study the object. He frowns. It reminds him of the slingshot Gabby would use to shoot empty pop cans. But it isn't a slingshot. It's something he doesn't have words for.

"I'm gonna take Tao out of the seat an' put him on the ground. I want you to watch carefully, Kasper, 'cause what I do to him...you're gonna have to do it too."

*

The click of the belt's release. Then the stranger's arms sliding beneath his body. Tao feels his weight rise, fall. When his paws touch the ground he tries to run, but he is weak, minus a leg. He goes no farther than a stumble forward. The stranger has an iron grip on the skin folds behind his neck.

*

Kasper takes three deep breaths.

"Uh-oh. Oh no."

He shifts the headphones up, placing them over his eyes.

"Oh nooooo."

He shudders and pulls the headphones down again.

"Yeah, I know. This is unpleasant. But it's gotta be done. Grab his skin here, Kasper. Just like I'm doin'. Can you do that? Please? It's important. Please? Good, Kasper! That's it! Big chunk, yeah. Now hold on tight 'cause Tao's not gonna like what I'm about to do."

*

Boy's hand. Firm. Not as firm as the stranger, though. It isn't law. It isn't unconquerable. He could pull away, break the hold.

He won't.

He might hurt Boy.

Tao recalls the recent past: the kickstart to their escape when biting Boy was a brief consideration. He had neither the fortitude nor the promise of success to follow through. And regardless of the situation's futility, what horror would ensue from leaving Boy alone now that the human is armed?

He looks at the cuffed jeans and the dirty sneakers. Listens to the low hum. He doesn't blame Boy for the punishment to come. Boy is slow. And just following orders.

Such is life for the low-born.

*

Grasping the clutch of skin and hair, Kasper is reminded of the wigs he wore with the occupational therapist. His palm prickles. Goosebumps dot his forearm. His free hand cradles his jaw. The tip of his index finger brushes his earlobe, ready to dart into the canal if there is whining or yelping.

"I'm sorry… So-so sorry."

"Forgive me too, Tao. This is the way it's gotta be."

*

A bomb detonates in Tao's injured leg, obliterating his lower body. His heart stutters. Ragged breaths tear at his lungs. He opens his mouth wide. Ropes of drool reach for the dry grass. The growls and the snarls stuck in the depths of his throat are too great to be swallowed or set free. His front legs shake as if reeling from a poison pellet.

Boy's hold. Despite the tumult, he feels the fingers on his neck loosen, then release. With blurred vision, Tao sees Boy's sneakers shift from beside his front left paw to beneath his snout. Knees bend and touch the ground. Hands tap the thighs.

An age passes before the agony releases. Tao's body slides back into the dull ache and thrumming itch it knew before the explosion. He wants to slump down, roll over, but submission gives licence, permits passage. He must stand between the stranger and Boy. He must endure.

Tao hesitates to look behind. More punishment is coming; it never ceases after a single blow—the tortured dogs told him so. Against his better judgement, he peeks over his left shoulder.

The stranger stands at the stroller, wiping his hands and nodding his head. He collects a dirty rag from one of the side pockets and wipes his face. Then he bunches the cleanest corner of the rag and dabs at his cone-covered ears.

Tao blinks, sending the stranger's cleanup into the background and bringing his wounded leg into focus. It is no longer bent—knee, heel and paw are aligned. Pressed against the side of the leg, running parallel, is the weapon. A harness has secured it to his hips and rump. Three strips of grey tape bind it to the limb.

Cautiously, he lowers the leg. The tip of the weapon touches down, paw suspended an inch above the ground. Tao leans on the makeshift support. There is no great hurt atop the ache and the itch. He looks forward again. Boy still kneels before him. Tao drops down onto his belly.

*

Kasper rubs his hands. Then he places them palm down over the dog's resting head. He moves them back and forth, from nose to ears and back again.

No contact, always an inch of separation.

"That's a pretty decent splint, Tao. Yeah. Should help a lot. You know, I didn't come here lookin' for that—I was lookin' for some dog medicine or animal medicine, something to help you with the pain. Not that I thought I'd find anythin', yeah. This place been looted like a bank vault, same as everywhere else. But you never know. Maybe there'd be somethin' lyin' around that everyone missed. An' what do you know, I found that! In one of the crates left behind, yeah. Good bit of luck. Couldn't find any bandages, though—no surprise. So I had to use duct tape. Fixes anythin', duct tape. Even messed-up legs."

The man removes his faded raincoat and ties it around his waist. He runs the back of his hand across his perspiring brow.

"I think we should celebrate you gettin' back on all fours, Tao. Let's eat. It's on me, yeah."

*

The trio wander around to the rear of the ruined veterinary clinic, searching for seclusion, flat ground and shade. They find all three beneath a blood-red Freeman maple, standing sentry in right field of an overgrown baseball diamond. The man lifts several food items from the stash in his stroller. The dog's meal—a can of chunky slop, a far cry from the hypoallergenic kibble that was, until the rationing, his two squares a day with Family—is barely on the ground before it is gone. The boy takes his time, sniffing packets, assessing textures, eating one crumb after another.

High above the feast, the sun ghosts toward the western horizon. Night will envelop the town in a few hours. A cloudless sky, free of streetlights, will host a thousand stars and a polished crescent moon. The few who still look up in wonder will be grateful for the spectacle, and for the reminders: there are people living beyond fear and hate and primal instinct, there are places in the world that aren't devouring themselves, there are distant planets under the reign of eternal silence, there is an infinite universe dedicated to spotlighting the gift of humanity. They will look up needless of a reminder that they are nothing.

If the clouds persist, night will be darker than the wings of a swallowtail.

*

An unfamiliar friend: comfort.

The desert mirages of ten minutes before were actual oases. Fear of the stranger? Unfounded. The weapon? A bringer of relief rather than turmoil. Sacrificing himself for Boy? Perhaps another time. Best of all, his stomach is no longer empty. It is not full, either.

Tao cranes his neck, hoping for more to eat. The stranger, leaning back against the tree, is not receptive. Head tilted down, mask discarded, bottle of pungent liquid in the lap. Cloth held against one ear then the other. Tao shifts his attention to Boy, sitting cross-legged on the grass. Food in the right hand, resting on the right knee. Attention divided between the crimson leaves surrounding and a dragonfly drifting on the breeze. There is potential here, as there always was at home.

A drop. A spill. A snack forgotten and left within reach. He positions his head by Boy's right sneaker and waits for the right moment.

*

Kasper feels the breath on his shin. With side-eye, he observes the dog rise to his feet, staring at his right hand.

"Uh-oh."

Nose sniffing. Closing in.

"Tao, no eat!"

Tongue swiping, catching a corner of the packet.

"TAO, NO EAT!"

Kasper crams the snack into his mouth, chews it up and, with eyes shut tight, swallows. He folds the packaging and stuffs it in his jeans pocket.

"Wow, if looks could kill." The stranger cough-laughs then takes a sip from his bottle. "Tao's not very happy with your lack of generosity there, Kasper. Might be best if you two separate for a bit. Hey, I know you been eyein' the little playground just past the bleachers over there. Wanna go mess around? Looks in pretty good shape, not too damaged. Come."

*

Headphones bouncing at his neck, the boy bounds along a rickety rope bridge, then negotiates a climbing wall with half of its rocks missing. Man and dog look on from a concrete bench, posted at the apex of the playground's triangular, mostly intact rubber matting.

"*T-A-O*. You know what that means, yeah?" The stranger smirks at the resulting stare, the cocked head, the ears at attention. "*Tao* means 'the way,' 'the path.'"

He looks to the south and the cityscape, a steel lesion on the skin of the land. Great plumes of black smoke stain the sky like the ink of a kraken.

"This is my path. Not sure where it's leadin'. Just know I need to keep puttin' one foot in front of the other, yeah. Like my tours with Squad—I knew if I kept puttin' one foot in front of the other, I'd make it home.

That was the place I was tryin' to get to: home." He turns back to the dog and gives him a scratch behind the ear. "You got a path, Tao? You have a place you're tryin' to get to? Can't imagine you do."

He eases down off the bench and wraps his arms around the dog's neck.

*

He watches Kasper ride the slide, arms raised, *The Gingerbread Man* held high.

"The first folks the Nazis killed were the disabled. Did you know that, Tao?"

Laying on his side at the man's feet, the dog stretches and grunts.

"Not many people know that, yeah. They were the guinea pigs for the injections, the gas chambers. 'Unworthy lives,' they called them. The Nazis got the idea from some German doctor in the twenties. He did a survey, asked parents of disabled kids if they'd be okay with their children dyin' during the course of his experiments. You want to guess what percentage said they'd be cool with that?"

Tao blinks.

"Seventy-three. Seventy-three said it would be okay. But under one condition: so long as they were never told about it. Can you believe that? Go ahead and kill my kid, just don't let it be on my conscience, yeah. Seventy-three fuckin' percent."

Tao blinks again.

"Now, this chump in charge today, an' the Reparation Party... Are they as bad as the Nazis? I remember during the pandemic there was talk of disabled folks bein' denied hospital beds an' ventilators, but it wasn't official policy. So, is it fair to compare 'em to the Nazis? The protestors were sure callin' 'em Nazis from day one—I don't know if that's accurate. Don't get me wrong, these people are bad. Real bad. I mean, look around—they pitted people against one another until the country tore itself apart. But Nazis? The absolute worst of the worst in history? I'm not even sure they're as bad as some of the grunts beside me when I was in Squad."

He nods in the direction of Kasper, now playing with a set of tic-tac-toe blocks. The boy arranges it in his usual way: the centre *O* surrounded on all sides by *X*s.

"Our young friend here is a good example—he's still alive. Still kickin', yeah. The Nazis would've killed him in the first five minutes. The Reparation Party, at least they got a trace of pity. An' here's the thing: Kasper needs that pity. There's none out here on the streets, not with the pretend Homers runnin' wild. I figure Kasper's only lasted this long 'cause of you, Tao. But lastin' as long as you can... that's not a plan. That's not a path. No offence, our young friend needs human beings helpin' him out. An' it can't be me. I can't take on that kind of burden. The Defs? The good guys? Where are they? No one's seen a lick of them lately. An' anyway, they want soldiers not charities. They don't want fifteen-year-old kids who can't do anythin' 'cept quote from a child's book."

The man reaches over to the stroller, unhooks the restraint on the radio and sets it down on the bench as if it were a priceless antique. He exhales and removes the cone from his right ear. Then he cleans the canal with a black fingernail, gritting his teeth through every scrape.

"No, this is Kasper's best path," he says, wiping the fingernail on his raincoat before flipping the radio's power switch. "His only path."

*

"Is that Captain Shore?... I want to talk to Captain Shore... Drew Colborn... *D-R-E-W-C-O-L-B-O-R-N*... He knows who I am, he gave me this line, yeah... Ex-military, Black Halo Squad... I don't give a shit about your 'thank you for my service'—I want you to get a message to Captain Shore. Tell him I have someone to exchange, someone that's escaped processin'... A boy... No, he's not—he's actually retarded... I don't know what he's got... He can't have a conversation, doesn't have a clue what's going on... Maybe fifteen years old... No family from what I can make out... No, no connection to the Defiance, he's out here on his own... I actually think he's a good opportunity for you lot, yeah. Show the people your softer side, the people you haven't killed or kicked out or jailed for their own 'protection' that is ... What do I want? The usual: supplies, assurances, medicine for my ears ... My ears—they're hurtin' like hell ... Shore gave me somethin' last time ... Whatever you got, I'll take it ... We good? ... Okay then ... On Grigson Street, halfway down ... Check the old maps—there was a vet clinic here. We're just behind it, at a little playground ... How long? ... Ten minutes, okay ... I'll be here with my dog ... An' hey, tell 'em to go easy on the boy, okay? ... Tell 'em to go easy—don't forget ..."

The stranger shuts off the radio, returns it to the stroller seat. He shifts his attention to the playground in time to see Kasper leap off of the swing, plant a two-footed landing and shout, "TA-DAH!" He applauds. Then he bends over to address the prone dog, gnarled hands on knees.

"I'm sorry, Tao. You're goin' to have to get trussed up again. Can't have you runnin' free when the Homers arrive, especially now you got a fourth leg again. Come on—up you get."

*

Tao gets to his feet as the stranger prepares the seat belt. The scene playing out is disorienting. His leg is okay—the best it's been since he awoke this morning. Why would the chair be needed? Is the weapon about to be taken away? Is he soon to be left alone again?

"You know my Márquez book?" he says, bending at the knees. "It's about death, but it's just as much about love."

Contact on his belly—the stranger's hands. But not only there. On his back, a soft touch. A kiss, a caress. Then an embrace. Familiar affection. Warmth provided, but not by skin and sinew and bone. Rather, linen and polyester.

The jacket.

Returned.

As Tao is lifted off the ground, he doesn't know why he wears the uniform again or what has prompted its appearance. He only knows that an effect will take hold, a happening will reveal his course of action.

The stranger places him in the stroller seat and straps him in. Perhaps cued by the click of the seat belt, the murmurs of a distant siren commence.

"Just because love isn't there at the beginning, doesn't mean it can't be there at the end."

No physical gift. No sage voice of Trainer. Beyond surprise and anticipation, Tao feels no different. The siren grows louder, its murmur now chatter. His clenching stomach knows: it's not headed elsewhere, not the farms or the docks or the scarcely beating heart of the village. The siren is coming for them. It is the withdrawing sea that will soon engulf them as a tsunami.

Tao wriggles and pulls, impatient with the inertia. They need to go, to hide. Where is the stranger's haste? The clapping hands? The hustling feet? The urgent push of the stroller? The barked commands to Boy? He whines.

The stranger shakes his head. "Over time, love can be earned an' learned."

Tao shrinks in his seat.

The face of the stranger has vanished. Nose, mouth, ears, beard—wiped away. In their place, a surface as plain and delicate and featureless as an eggshell.

"Tao, you'll love me in the end."

Only the ears and their cardboard conches remain.

"I know you will."

The siren is upon him now. Prying open his muzzle, digging into the back of his throat.

If you and the boy are to have a chance
You must respond, Tao
You must answer

*

At last, he feels it.

The jacket opening, expanding like a birth canal. Feeding his lungs with the air of the ancients, filling his throat with the light of the moon. Fuelling his tongue to counter the strafing siren.

He looks to the sky, purses his mouth.

And howls.

Loud.

Long.

Without pause.

Without breath.

Sound waves pound the playground and adjoining field. The grass bends. The ground shrugs. Trees shiver, littering the dry dirt with a rainbow of fall colours.

The stranger cries out and claws at the cones, sending them spinning to the ground. Blood pours from his ears, the hands thrust against them helpless to stem the flow. A reach for Tao is severed as the howl climbs to a higher register. The knees buckle. The body lists to one side, then collapses. The stranger writhes on the ground, floundering in a pool of red.

And suddenly Boy is there. Face half-turned, shoulders twitching, mouth forming an *O*. Headphones on. Mimicking the moans of the fallen stranger. Still baying, Tao pushes against the belt, extending his right front leg. At the end of the leg is not the paw he recognizes, but a hand. Four fingers and a thumb sprouting from a smooth hairless palm. It grasps Boy's own hand and brings it down, placing it on the clasp of the restraint.

*

Kasper stands on tiptoe and presses the small red button with the knuckle of his thumb.

The seat belt bursts open.

*

With freedom, the stretched elastic of Tao's perception rebounds back to reality.

His howl subsides.

His paw reforms.

His back is stripped of the jacket, bare as the day he left the program.

*

Kasper claps as Tao scrabbles out of the stroller. He lifts *The Gingerbread Man* from his jeans and holds it out.

"Take, Tao."

The dog takes the book in his mouth and sets off before the command can be repeated.

*

They run.

Quicker than before. Tao's splint is strong; though the damaged leg is far from an asset, it is no longer slowing his progress. Kasper keeps up, ignoring the distractions: an overturned wheelbarrow, a dumpster on fire, seagulls squabbling over the grisly contents of a sleeping bag. No half skips in his stride.

They run.

Down side alleys. Through gaps in fences. Past bodies punched with holes and open pits half filled. With every detour, every diversion, the siren follows, its wail constant, its pursuit relentless. Dog and boy are on borrowed time now that the hounds have picked up their scent.

But fate is patient, preferring the facade of a fair fight. On Buckminster Road, as they approach the entry to the Spirit Walk trail, the siren fades. And then it's gone, slipped back into the lengthening shadows of the late afternoon.

8

I stood in the centre of the room, hands behind my back like a cuffed criminal. Jay leaned against the doorway. At our feet, Kasper thrashed on the floor, red faced, shouting.

"Try the hammock again?" he asked, folding his arms and raising his voice above the din.

I shook my head. "He's too far gone. And it's too risky for us to try and lift him in there."

"How about 'What's Going On'?"

"Can't play a song without electricity or batteries. You'll have to sing it, Marvin."

"Eh, he's suffering enough."

I offered a thin smile. We would've laughed five years ago, two years ago. Maybe even six months ago. Not now. Like all other life essentials, sense of humour had been rationed.

"The weighted blanket?"

"He tore it last week, remember?"

"Right." He rubbed his eyes. "What'll we do?"

"I have no clue."

I knelt and stroked our son's trembling back. He kicked his legs, narrowly missing my chest and shoulder.

"I can't take this. I'm going out."

"Where?"

"The store. Maybe they've got a box of his crackers."

"They haven't had them for weeks. They haven't had much of anything for weeks."

"Maybe we'll get lucky. Or maybe getting out of here for a few minutes I can think straight and come up with some other way to calm him down."

"Be really careful. Hurry back."

"Curfew's still an hour away."

"Yes, it is. Be really careful and hurry back."

He kissed the top of my head, winced at Kasper's anguished moan and hustled from the room. Seconds later, Gab appeared in the corridor, wearing armour she'd made of cardboard and tinfoil. Tao at her side sported a glittery collar and helmet. The name printed in elaborate cursive on her sword: Time Slayer.

"Is Kasper okay, Mom?"

"Not just at this moment, honey."

"I caught my hand in the screen door earlier. I cried a bit. He must have heard."

"It's not your fault when this happens. It's no one's fault."

"Yes it is."

"Sorry?"

"It's the Riparation's fault."

"Reparation. With an E*."*

She knighted the dog with the sword. "I know, Mom. I say it with an I *because then it's the* R-I-P*-aration, which means they're marked for death."*

"Where on earth did you get that from?"

"Our music teacher, Mr. Pau. He used to say it every class. Until he left school."

"Where did he go?"

"I don't know. Mrs. Thielmann, the new music teacher, didn't tell us."

"Uh-huh."

"I don't like Mrs. Thielmann—she doesn't smile or laugh or joke around at all. She looks grumpy all the time."

"Yeah well, don't be saying that R-I-P *stuff to her. Don't say it anywhere but in this house. And you know what, don't say it too loud here."*

"Okay."

"As for your brother, he'll be fine. We just need to find something that'll help him calm down."

"Mom?"

"Yes, Gab."

"I feel the same as Kasper sometimes. On the inside."

I stood and hugged her. "I do too, honey. And Dad. It's going to get better, though. I promise."

"You promise?"

"Cross my heart and hope to R-I-P*-aration."*

She patted the sword's plastic hilt and trotted down the staircase, Tao in tow.

The same as Kasper sometimes. It was true—at this moment, on the floor screaming in frustration, begging for some measure of relief, some glimmer of hope that madness could be overcome and joy restored, our son represented the whole family. Hell, the whole country. Okay, the percentage of the country—God, let it be the majority—that still clung to respect and decency as their bookends. Kasper's refusal to go quietly into the night was a blow struck for resistance. Protestors witnessing his meltdown would've applauded.

A pyrrhic victory, of course. There weren't any exceptions with this regime. Disability wasn't a licence to rage. An IQ below seventy-five didn't give you a free pass for dissent. After curfew, a meltdown was just another prompt for an anonymous call to the authorities.

The irony—Kasper treated the same as everyone else.

The shrieks, for a time abiding by an uneasy truce, exploded like a grenade, the shrapnel tearing through me and lodging in my soul. Dazed and nauseous, I sat down on the bed. It was hopeless now. Forty minutes of bargaining, cajoling, mitigating... vaporized in a flash. Nothing left but survival instinct. I fumbled up a book from the pile on the floor, clawed it open to the first page. With as much volume as my vocal cords could muster, I read aloud: "Once upon a time, there lived an old man, an old woman and a little boy. On this day, the old woman was baking. With the dough that was left over, she made a gingerbread man with the help of the little boy..."

I eased down onto my side, facing the wall, back to my son. The book shared the pillow, propped in my trembling wrists and fingers.

"The gingerbread man had two black currants for eyes, a red cherry for a nose, a green apple slice for a mouth and three purple grapes for buttons on his shirt..."

I read four more pages before I realized: I could hear myself. The shouting was mine alone. I went to roll over, then stopped.

"... Run, run, fass as you can... You can't catch me, I'm the Ginnerbread Man."

A brush of skin on my upper left arm. The creak of the wooden bed slats under a hundred and thirty pounds of additional weight. Finally, undeniable proof of the salvage: a warm body snuggling mine, a hand on my hip, whistly breaths on the back of my neck.

Tears seized my eyes. Tremors claimed my chin. Choking sobs streamed single file into my chest. I let the mighty wave build and crest and then, as it crashed down, I dived under, holding my breath and kicking my legs. When I surfaced, I wiped my eyes and my nose. Filled my lungs.

The rest of the book I read in a whisper.

Escape has sidetracked Tao and Kasper to the lip of the town where land meets Gilder Reach. As they run and hide and hide and run, they meet with less destruction in this section of the map. Trees and traffic lights upright. Houses untouched. Streets largely free of debris. Tippett & Sons Gun Shop on River Drive is business as usual, its neon Open sign glowing like a cigarette end in the sepia light of dusk.

Passing by the docks, they stare at the gaggle of unmolested vessels, mostly military, some luxury. A forty-five-foot yacht called *Gravy Boat* is the pride of the small fleet.

*

Their first encounter with a crowd comes at the waterfront pub, Steeds. An assortment of trucks and cars occupy the dirt parking lot. Four of the parked vehicles have Homeland Union Security Headquarters decals. Inside, there are lights on. Though the doors and windows of the pub are closed, the noise can be heard from a distance. Shouting. Music. The occasional breaking of glass.

Across the street, crouching in the dike that fronts the collapsed facade of Berg's Hardware Store, Tao and Kasper watch as two men and a woman emerge from the pub. Each wears a brown uniform that has seen better days. Pants low on the hips. Shirts untucked and open at the chest. The woman is in the middle of the trio, barely conscious, arms draped over the shoulders of the men. Her head lolls to one side and her bare feet drag on the pavement. Despite her wretched state, she is a conqueror flaunting the spoils of war: Rolex watch, Cuban white-gold chain, hand-sewn Napoleon hat plucked from the head of a Defiance traitor.

The carriers bring the woman to the nearest Homeland vehicle, open a door and deposit her in the back seat. One of the men starts to shut the door but is stopped by the other. A heated discussion takes place. If it is heard in the pub, no one is moved to investigate. The argument lasts several minutes until one of the men—older and smaller in stature than the other—pushes his colleague aside and slams the door shut. He tucks in his shirt, marches back to the pub's entrance and disappears inside. The bigger man shouts and gestures, then glances around the parking lot. He presses against the car window, hands cupping his face for a clearer view. After a time, he stands up straight and traces the footsteps of the older man back to the entrance. He stares one last time at the car, then slips out of view.

Staying low in the dike, Tao and Kasper move past Steeds and on toward the battered village centre.

*

At the top of Main Street, Tao takes a breather on the porch of the boarded-up Bait & Tackle Shop. This could be a moment to savour small victories. They've made it this far. They are on course again, the line between here and the training facility close to gun-barrel straight. The imminent night promises easier hiding. They are together. They are alive.

Tao, though, is not inclined toward a jump or a spin or a tail wag. His stomach squirms from the stranger's canned slop. The raw blotches on his skin are multiplying. The weapon has revealed its underbelly; at the spot where the grey tape is highest on his leg, the hair has worn away and a small crescent of blood is taking shape. The physical adversaries are great—yet, it is the mind's weariness that scratches at his soul.

The stranger was bad.

The stranger was not a friend.

He didn't see.

He put Boy in danger.

Failure weighs on Tao's ninety-pound frame like a collapsed beam. The sense of duty remains strong, but commitment is wasted effort without the tools necessary to succeed. Does he possess them? Only when he wears the jacket, hears the voice of Trainer, it seems. Back in the program, he lost them. How long before he loses them again? In their absence, what will be at his disposal if he once more mistakes foe for friend?

He looks at Boy sitting on the porch beside him, legs crossed, staring at one hand as if it were a creature thought extinct. Tao recognizes the difficult truth delivered by the masked stranger: as it was five years ago, he is ill-equipped to guide, to lead, to save. He does not stand above. He is below.

Like Boy, he is lesser.

*

Rouselle's Boutique.

Sip Coffee House.

Gilder Village Dentist.

Taverna Terzopoulos.

The Thrift Store.

When Main Street wasn't a looter's checklist, Kasper regularly visited as part of his class's community access. He liked the outings—the movement, the fresh air, the open space that dispersed sound rather than concentrating it within four walls. He enjoyed the predictability of the route and the faces. The greetings.

Passing by the gutted remains of Delmano's Restaurant, he slows and lifts a headphone. The slide pulled from his memory deck: the hail of the tall man who smells like cheese and sounds like he is speaking through a microphone. He waits for the greeting. Then he walks on, unrewarded.

At each of his former checkpoints, Kasper is faithful to the routine: slow, lift, remember, wait, walk on. At the end of Main Street, he takes three deep breaths.

*

On the corner of the Trunk Road and Arsenault Drive, Kasper pauses and taps his thigh. He has arrived at another nook he knows well from community access. Pet's Place. The Traveller. Gilder Gospel Assembly. And diagonally across the intersection, behind an uprooted katsura tree, The Village Clinic. Once upon a time, his favourite stop of all.

"Ooooh lookit Kasper," he murmurs. "Is your mom."

Through the early evening gloom, he traces over the picture of damage done. Windows smashed. The front door in pieces on the brown-green grass, twenty feet from its frame. A treatment table lying on its back near the sidewalk. Apples in various states of rot on the ground, a feast for a cadre of crows.

"Your mom, Kasper. She works there. Sheezat the window, see?"

Broken bodies, heaped like laundry, block the red brick path running parallel to the clinic. A head sits to the right of the pile, propped on its bloody neck, facing the dormant street.

"Sheez in the window waving atchoo, Kasper. Giff her a wave."

He frowns, shakes his head. The thigh taps have escalated to a white-knuckled drum.

"Go on. Gif her a wave."

He squeezes his eyes shut. Tears glitter like mica powder on the tips of his lashes.

"Whatta big smile, Kasper. You are soo haaappy to see your momma."

He lifts *The Gingerbread Man* from the back of his jeans, holds it at his waist and stares at the front cover as he crosses the street.

"Okay, time-to-go now. Say bye-bye. Bye-bye."

Thirty strides down Arsenault Drive, the clinic slips out of sight, lost in the paper birches lining the sidewalk. He tucks the book back into his jeans. He wipes his eyes with the back of his hand, then wipes the back of his hand on a curbside bench and its faded, defaced realtor ad.

*

They reach the modest campus of Gilder High. The digital sign is damaged beyond repair. The front gate that featured two limestone pillars, each inscribed with the initials *GH*, is a pile of rubble. The mass of anti-Reparation-Party graffiti on the pavement leading to the administration office is gone, covered by tar and gravel or doused in white paint. The school motto on the mural—"Take Every Stride With Panther Pride!"—reads "Fake Every Lie With Ranter Pride!" The odour of decaying flesh is strong, but there are no visible corpses.

Tao scans the scene. Despite the desolation, echoes still ring. This is where the voices were loudest. Uncivil. Unapologetic. Speaking the names. Taunting the hounds. Shouting the words their masters dared not say. Crying out as the bodies fell.

He considers Boy standing on tiptoe beside a crushed bike frame lying in the weeds. Headphones around the neck. Fingers in the ears. He knows this was Boy's training facility, the place for learning. Why here? A site that spurned silence? Surely it was a mistake. Surely, like him, Boy couldn't meet the expectations of the trainers and was destined to fail. And yet, they must have been kind to Boy because there is no anger or sadness or disgust in the eyes. Only something approaching love.

Tao walks on a few yards, turns and sits down. Time to go, Boy. This might've been a safe place once, but not anymore. He looks for the sign. After a brief wait, it comes.

*

Kasper bends down, lifts the Velcro straps on his sneakers, pulls them tighter, then presses them back into place. He stands and straightens his back. Places his right hand over his heart. Quietly sings.

"Momma, momma...There's too minny off you crying...Brother, brother...There's afar too minny off you dying...Tok to mee, so you can seeee...Oh, wuzz going on...Wuzz going on...Yes, wuzz going on... Wuzz going on."

He lifts his headphones back onto his ears and returns to Tao on the Arsenault tarmac.

*

Ten hours since their escape. How many more to go? Another ten? Twenty? Fifty? Minutes and seconds have lost all meaning. Steps are the measure of time, each one bringing closer a midnight unknown.

Walk awhile. Rest. Drift like lifeboats at sea. Duck beneath the swaying feet of a man hanged from a makeshift gallows. Lap at the last dribbles of a broken fire hydrant run dry.

*

Cedar hedges reduced to spindly black skeletons serve as the backdrop for road signs pocked with bullet holes. Wires hang from listing poles like dead vines. They see little of it—not due to the failing light, but because this is the world now, the norm. Sights granted a stay of execution are more likely to catch the eye.

With each step, the village peters out and the farms near. To supporters of the Reparation Party, houses in this corner of Gilder were obscene. Multiple storeys, grand extensions. Circular driveways that accommodated expensive cars. A clear measure of darkened doors and stolen dreams. In truth, the homes symbolized struggle rather than excess. They sheltered many—grandparents, uncles, aunts, cousins. Rooms often bare, cardboard boxes serving as furniture and beds. The expensive cars? To save face. A chin held high to the country that thwarted every effort at betterment. None of it mattered to the Reps. The houses were an affront to everything they held dear and, as such, singled out for special treatment.

Today, dog and boy shamble past them without so much as a glance. With good reason—they are not there. Every stone, every brick, every stud is gone. Land cleared. Foundations extracted. Driveways covered with dirt.

*

Pop-pop-pop-pop-pop

They dart into the front yard of a half-demolished bungalow and hide behind the columns on the porch. A truck carrying a dozen Homeland officers wheels into view, headed east. Then another. And another. Five in all. Headlights ablaze, flashers on. As they pass, several point to the sky.

Pop-pop-pop-pop-pop

A large semi sweeps by, its trailer a long crate with many portholes. Tao sniffs the air. Piss and shit and sweat, and the twin stenches of confusion and dread. Animals to the slaughter. But they aren't animals.

A further three cars bring up the rear. As the last rounds the bend, an understanding finds Tao: apart from the semi, the vehicles' only sound is a whisper. Some make no sound at all. Without the sirens, you wouldn't know they were there.

*

At the Schenn Street intersection, Tao throws up.

The violence of the spasms is beyond anything he can recall from his past—barbed knots shredding his guts then cleaving his throat in two. At its height, he thinks this is it: the quest is over, his undoing complete. Will Boy stay with him until the darkness falls? But the thoughts are expelled with the last spits of stomach acid and half-digested food.

He pants, trying to cool his tongue. He looks at the puddle he has made. Instantly, there is a keening in his bowels, an urge to fill the void. He starts to sniff the mess when the crunch of gravel pricks his ears.

Boy has left his side and is backed up against the street sign, body in a semi-crouch. Eyes wide. Breathing fast. Finger pointed to the opposite sidewalk. Tao turns. A pack of dogs has emerged from an alley, five in all, an assortment of shapes, sizes and breeds. The alpha is a female German shepherd in her prime.

Tao's mind races. Run? Boy is too scared to move. Hide? Pointless. They see us. And they smell the terror—Boy reeks of primal fear. Tao moves to a spot in front of the street sign and sits facing the oncoming pack. He wants a look at the alpha's face, but a combination of the encroaching dusk and the lingering brain haze of the retching prevents a clear view.

The pack forms a semicircle around them. One of the dogs—a young border collie—stands with a paw raised and teeth bared. The alpha growls and the collie sits, tucks his head into his shoulders and turns toward the street. Tao bends low and takes a small step forward. Behind him, there is a moan.

It's okay, Boy. I'm with you. I'm not going anywhere.

The alpha paces back and forth, gaze fixed on Tao. Then she approaches. Slowly, but without hesitation. Behind her the dogs lean in, ready for a command issued or an action required. Tao stays low as she inspects him, then stock-still as she begins to nudge and prod. Again, there is a moan in back.

Calm, Boy. Be calm.

The alpha is careful, thorough. No area uncharted, no risk unaccounted for. For a brief moment, she breaks away to examine the nearby pool of vomit. Then she is back, directly facing Tao. Her tail buzzes. The pack dials down and starts exploring the sidewalk.

Tao noses up under the alpha's muzzle and licks her neck—the prelude to an exchange in the visceral language of the ancients.

*

What are you doing here?

I am taking the young human to a safe place.

There is no safe place.

I believe there is one.

We have yet to see it.

I believe.

You are tired.

Yes.

And unwell.

Yes.

And still you guide a stranger?

He is not a stranger. He is Family.

He is scared.

Yes.

Of us.

He's always been uncomfortable around us. Around me.

*

The shepherd shifts her attention to Kasper. She angles toward him, zigging left, zagging right. She circles him, feeling his cowardice, noting the book clutched to his chest, wondering at the strange coverings on his ears. She sniffs a sneaker.

*

He is odd. And weak.

He is not the same as other humans. He needs help.

Must it come from you?

There is no one else.

*

She returns to her previous position fronting Tao. The pack leaves its distractions and gathers around her. In the western sky, lost in a grey canopy of cloud, the sun recuses itself as witness and dips beneath the horizon.

*

Leave the young human and come with us.

I cannot.

You wish to live?

Yes.

Then come with us.

I cannot abandon Family.

We are your family. We will give you strength again. Continue on your current journey and it will not end well.

I have a duty.

*

Restlessness in the pack—hanging tongues and twitching noses and hunching shoulders. The alpha is not finished, but her gaze has shifted from the exchange now. She has eyes only for Boy.

*

I served a young human. She was not odd or weak. She was strong, in body and mind. I loved her. I thought we would defeat the violence and the chaos. But she was no match for the hounds. They put a hole in her chest and in her head. I stayed with her until they took her away.

It is the way of the world. It is the way of this world. If the strong cannot survive, what chance do the odd and the weak have? Your young human will die. And it will be a mercy.

Come with us.

*

Tao looks over his shoulder. Before his vision lands on Boy, he knows what he'll see. Hands over the face. Curled, shaking body near to the ground. Lips thin, absorbing a quiet hum of surrender.

It will be a mercy.

Before madness swallowed the world, he knew what mercy meant: failure without fear, words without weapons. The things Family never denied him despite his inadequacy: walking together, eating well, sleeping under a roof. From time to time there was punishment—stern faces and angry sounds and banishment outside—but it was always temporary, never permanent. Mercy was predictable, understood. Often restorative. It was a comfort greater than the smell of Woman in the cushions of the couch, or the rub of Girl's hands on his rib cage.

Mercy.

It means something different now.

Tao takes a step away from Boy.

Then two more.

A ripple of excitement runs through the pack.

*

A memory. Times with the other training dogs at the off-leash park. The freedom was exhilarating, but short-lived. More than once he imagined the fences gone. He and the others would run and run and not look back, not even for the commands of Trainer.

*

Tao stops and turns. He stands beside the alpha. Fifteen feet away, Boy is on the ground, sideways, knees drawn to the chest. The hands still cover the face. The hum has ended.

Mercy—it means something different.

But it should never lose all meaning.

*

I cannot.

*

The alpha exhales through her nose. She looks up at the sky. No moon, no stars. Just the grey bruises of a thousand clouds.

Soon, they will be black.

*

What if he were to die now?

*

Behind the alpha, the pack paws at the ground, growling as one. Foam gathers at the corners of the border collie's seething mouth.

Tao blinks. His stomach is lurching again. Blood pounds the shorelines of his inner ears. Bones in every corner of his body creak and groan in anticipation.

He grunts.

*

You will not harm Boy. I still possess the jacket, the Trainer's voice. And if I must, I will die in Boy's defence.

*

The alpha yawns, then fronts Tao, blocking his path to Kasper. She licks her chops, then leans to one side. The supported leg—she saw it during their introduction. Misshapen, streaked with blood. Such a poor foundation for fight or flight. She stretches and nods.

The signal.

Tao pivots, ready to repel the attack. He finds only bare asphalt. He scans the opposite sidewalk in time to see the pack disappear into a thicket of boxwood. He turns back to the alpha. She leans in and nuzzles his neck.

*

I wish you well.

*

He watches the shepherd bound across the road and through the thicket. When his heart settles back into the centre of his chest, he approaches the fetal heap at the foot of the street sign.

Rise, Boy.

He pokes his nose in the crack between the exposed elbow and rib cage. There's a flinch. And a surprise—a giggle. He digs in a second time. Jerks of delight and a snort of laughter.

"No, Tao! No tickle!"

*

Kasper sits up. He wears a smile, but it can't hide the residual hue of terror. His cheeks are wet. Eyes are rimmed with red. The headphone on his left ear has twisted forward, bending the cartilage. *The Gingerbread Man* remains pinned to his breast.

He breathes deep then reaches out, palm down, over the dog's head. His mind argues for the established routine: run the hand over and along the spine, keep a constant separation. A thank you without the complication of contact. Like the "hugs" he would give visiting relatives—lean in, shoulder down, close enough to feel the heat of skin before pulling away.

Kasper blinks, then narrows his eyes to slits. He lowers his hand and pats Tao's head.

"Goo'boy."

*

Eight fifteen on a lost clock.

They reach the Submarine—the house unofficially representing the end of Gilder and the start of the farmlands, so named for its submerged structure of underground living spaces and its arrowhead roof sitting flush with the yard. Tao is uninterested in the Submarine and the fate of its occupants; whether they left or stayed, lived or died, whether the naturally fortified bunker became a war room for the local Defiance or an outpost of interrogation and torture for the Homeland forces. He only has eyes for the open spaces ahead.

The smells—so foreign from the ones that filled the white van on the way to training. Back then, hay and fertilizer and churned soil. Corn and potatoes and pumpkins and grapes and an array of berries almost too great to take in. Tonight they are mere spirits, haunting rather than inhabiting the breeze. In their place, a fug of chemicals and metals. And salt. Thick. Unremitting. Abrading the tongue with every breath.

A small whimper caroms around his throat. The earth's submission pains him in a way that is different than the loss of Family. Less devastating, but somehow deeper, as if a wasp were trapped in his bones, stinging his marrow. He sighs and stares down the angry red disc on his front left paw. His skin, like the land, is cracked and sore. Maybe beyond repair.

No time to waste, then.

With Boy at his heel, he plunges into the dark, wounded plains.

*

A storm on the stroke of nine o'clock. A torrential downpour that once belonged to other places, other skies. In tribute to the deniers, it is now a regular tourist here.

Kasper shifts *The Gingerbread Man* from the back of his jeans to the front, then bends forward, wearing the hard rain on his back and protecting the book. Every second step, he spits a single word of frustration:

"Wet!"

His shirt clings to his back. His jeans sag. Water drips from his hair, his nose, his elbows, the hinges of his headphones. He wants to take off his clothes, all of them, get rid of the damp and the cold and the ick that feels like seaweed on his skin. But exposing the book to the deluge—it's a risk too great to consider.

Kasper shakes his head. He starts to hum. Inside his sneakers and socks, his toes curl.

"WET! WET!"

*

Tao halts, backtracks to where Boy has come to a stop. In the darkness, he can't see the facial expressions. He doesn't have to—the urgent sounds and anxious movements tell him all he needs to know.

I am uncomfortable.

I need to be dry.

I cannot wait.

He saw this in Boy when Family went to the beach. In the water: shouts of delight, squeals of joy. Out of the water: shaking, frowning, Woman and Man scrambling to prevent a strip down to the naked form.

He looks around. No trees. They would only be temporary shelter anyway. A house? They are few and far between in this stretch. And what awaits under their roofs? More burned bodies? Another false friend? Hounds? Strays? Tao is unsure of what to do, where to go.

Until the decision is made for him.

*

Kasper runs.

Head down, leaning forward.

Legs pumping, arms across his chest.

*

Wait, Boy.

WAIT!

Tao barks then summons a sprint out of his weary frame. His busted leg drags, a pill once again, the splint no longer a relief. He stumbles into the black maw that swallowed Boy in an instant. For a few seconds, squelching shoes are his guide. The sound recedes. Fainter, fainter.

Then gone.

*

Panting and wide-eyed, the dog comes upon a ditched RV. The dented nose butts the bank of the shallow gully running parallel to the road; the back half of the vehicle nests on the shoulder. The large driver-side mirror hangs from its fractured wrist. Leaning against the rear wheel like a spare hubcap is the satellite dish from the roof. One of the rear tires is flat.

The door is open.

Tao listens. Something? Anything? Just rain pounding all around and his own puffing breath. Boy has to be inside though, because Boy stays. Boy doesn't leave without Family. Tao shakes off—the spray of water like a Catherine wheel—then climbs the step to the threshold of the coach.

The interior is unmarred. No debris or broken glass or fire damage. Two overhead storage compartments are open, but nothing has spilled out. The only object on the floor is an empty picture frame. A working flashlight on the kitchen counter casts a feeble glow over the ordered scene.

From the leftover smells, Tao doesn't think many people were here. Four, maybe five. A family, not unlike his own and not long gone. He senses their departure was hurried, fuelled by panic. They didn't pack—there was only time for each other. Hands joined, arms around shoulders. They left together, alone.

Boy sits at the small table, hunched over and trembling, teeth chattering. Naked apart from the headphones.

The face is calm.

*

Kasper lifts his head and squints at the blank TV in the cabinet. On the table, his wet clothes are heaped in a pile. His sneakers wade in a puddle on the laminate floor. *The Gingerbread Man* sits on the counter, dry but for a few spots on the cover.

From the corner of his eye, he watches Tao limp toward him, then drop at his bouncing feet. He burrows his frigid toes beneath the dog's damp but warm belly. After a time, his feet settle.

*

Bringing clothes to the master—it was one of the few tasks Tao could complete in training. In the controlled environment of a house or a room, away from the distractions of the outside world and relieved of the food retrieval duties his stomach could not abide, he got the job done. Sometimes the clothes made his nose prickle, and occasionally he would pause to sneeze. But he always delivered them into the necessary hands. Trainer was so very happy when he worked well. That made him happy.

Tao draws strength from the treasured memory as he searches the RV. Bunks. Toilet and shower. Kitchen. Queen bed. Beside the bed is a thin wardrobe and a small chest of drawers. He suspects they store clothes, but without a length of rope for him to bite and pull they are inaccessible. He wanders to the driver's side of the bed. Nothing useful on the floor or the small shelves. An empty plastic bottle. Two wire coat hangers. A rubber band. Coins litter the laminate—in the dim blush of the flashlight they glow like wary eyes. Tao starts to rest his chin on the edge of the bed, then stops short. Something under the pillow. He noses it aside and discovers reward for his effort: a pair of pyjamas. He takes them in his mouth and brings them back into the open space of the RV.

*

Eating!

Small nibbles of a sweet-smelling treat, jutting out of a packet peeled back. Similar to the food of the stranger. Where did it come from? When was it found? Boy must have discovered it while he was looking around the bed.

Tao's stomach starts its dance. Saliva collects at the edges of his mouth. He drops the pyjamas in Boy's lap and then sits, waiting for acknowledgement of his good work.

*

Kasper stands and places his snack on the counter, beside *The Gingerbread Man*, beyond the reach of the dog. He checks the pyjamas for wet patches. Finding none, he steps into the pants. Then he puts the shirt on backwards.

"Uh-oh," he says, giggling. "Oh no."

He claps and doubles over, the giggles escalating to laughter then breathless guffaws.

"Oh ... Nooo ... That's no gooood ... Try ... again!"

He lifts the shirt back over his head, replaces it the right way around. He thuds down onto the chair, gulping air and holding his stomach. It takes a minute or more for the laughter to completely die out.

*

Tao looks at Boy, at the snack, back at Boy. The energy he has left—it isn't enough to whine or beg.

He has barely enough to yawn.

*

The rain ends a few minutes before ten. An itch in Tao's gut demands a resumption of the journey. It was never his intention to sleep. Setting out, he figured, to push through until they reached the facility and then, with safety achieved, they could sleep all they wanted. Stay awake and on the move—it was a good plan. But now, inside the quiet and tidy welcome of the RV, his exhaustion is overwhelming.

With drowsy eyes, he looks around one last time. The door is closed shut—the wind at some point, no doubt. He limps over to the bunks. He likes the look of them, their inviting softness. And their trace smells remind him of Girl when she was small. He can't climb onto the bunks, though, not even the lower one. He doubts he has the strength to lift a front paw onto the mattress, let alone his whole body. He will make do with a warm, flat, dry patch of floor.

Boy is sitting on the lower bed, *The Gingerbread Man* propped in the left hand, turning pages with the right. No words. No sound. Far away, perhaps in another book, another story.

Tao folds his bad leg beneath his hips and eases down onto his side. Before the leg screams at being pinned between the weapon and his full weight, he rolls over.

*

He can see it.

The two of them arriving, walking under the sign and down the path to the office. Into the reception area where Paula at the Front Desk waits with a pat and a treat and a *Whoozagoodboy?* Then on past the delivery spaces and the nursery where the puppies are cared for; past the showers and the baths (the less thought given to these, the better). Due to the state of his leg and his skin and his stomach and everything else in his tumbledown body, he'll need to spend some time in the clinic with Doctor and the other gentle-handed humans. Maybe they'll be able to help Boy too. Then they'll enter the open areas: the cooler indoor space with line markings, the glorious grassed square with a roof overhead to catch the sun and the rain. And Trainer will be waiting there. And probably Assistants as well. Maybe some visiting humans, there to learn or to laugh or to feel better about their lives. Trainer will be very proud—Tao, the dog ill-equipped to guide, to lead, to save; burdened with being lower, being lesser; pitted against a world lost in a pall of death and destruction ... He came through. He delivered Boy to safety.

He imagines he might even get his jacket back.

*

Tao opens his eyes. For a second, he is unsure of his surroundings. Then it comes to him: Arsenault Drive, the farms, the abandoned RV. Nighttime. Darkness, save the flashlight on the table.

The presence at his back is new though.

A warm body snuggling. A hand on his hip. Whistly breaths on the back of his neck. He twists to look over his shoulder.

Impossibly, Boy is on the floor cradling him, fast asleep, the book a pillow for his head.

9

Patching a pair of old jeans, I looked up to see Gab fling the mangy tennis ball. Tao took off as if fired from a cannon, tongue trailing, legs a blur. He caught up with the rolling ball near the gate that opened onto Sixty-Eighth Street then trotted back, prize bulging the left side of his mouth.

"Nice, hon," I said. "Still got good heat."

She raised her thumb, then kissed her right bicep. She side-armed another throw into the yard, again sending the dog on his obligatory sprint.

Ten minutes a day, I thought. Better than no minutes at all. The ban on protests, the stricter curfew, the Homers' shutdown of Gilder High... all of it meant that good kids were unseen these days. Some of their fates I knew. Detained, deported. Arrested. Some just gone, vanished like a hiker in an avalanche. A good number—please God, a very good number—had gotten away and crossed the border, with family or without. Exactly how many was anyone's guess.

The ones still here and resisting the brainwash—they were laying low. A wise decision. Young people venturing more than a block from home were fodder for suspicious eyes and fearful whispers. One thing was certain: the blowhard in the big chair could no longer accuse the nation's youth of staying inside to mindlessly stare at their screens. Most of the screens were blank. And the ones that weren't had approved content 24-7.

I turned toward the house, listening for any hint of unhappiness. All quiet. No complaints. No distress. I exhaled. The return to the tech dark ages had been a tough transition for all of us, especially Kasper. At least some of his favourite things—puzzles, harmonica, The Gingerbread Man*—couldn't be taken away with the flick of a switch.*

And they couldn't take this away from Gab either. A ball, a dog, a bit of space. Ten minutes a day. Soon, she'd be able to do this without her mother having to stand guard.

We had an exit plan now.

Families with "retarded dependents" belonged to one of the few categories of citizenry being given permission to leave. A burden on the system, a drain on resources, unable to contribute to this great nation's rebuild—these were the justifications. Naturally, it was a different story for card-carrying members of the Reparation Party. Victims of Mother Nature's cruel vagaries, courageous parents inspiring us all to be better, families deserving of every support possible in their lifelong challenge. Fuck them. If they thought getting rid of the burdens and the drains with get-out-of-jail-free cards was winning the war, they were mistaken. This was only a battle. Winning the war was surviving the regime. Whatever it took.

I blinked, realizing I'd been staring at nothing. My renewed focus fell on Gab. She'd turned ninety degrees and was eyeing a small section of parking space between the townhouse blocks and alongside the driveway. At her hip, the dog was waiting for the next toss; Gab, though, was frozen in her throwing stance, ball held high, as if posing for a trophy cast. I followed her line of sight. Seeing the target, needle, thread and jeans fell from my lap onto the ground.

"Gabby, drop the ball! Open your hand, spread your fingers!"

I stood, my legs weak, barely capable of supporting my weight.

"Sweetheart, listen to me! Drop the ball and put both hands up, fingers spread!"

I looked again at the parking space. The Homeland car, black, stark, not a figment, not a night terror. Idling, but quieter than a dying breath. Likely two officers inside; the dark-tinted windows prevented any confirmation. No siren—just the yellow flashers spinning like mad eyes. When had it arrived? Where had it come from? I knew the answer: it had always been there.

Every atom of my body crying out, desperate to run, to grab, to hold, to hug, to shield, to protect. Tears gathering, spilling. I swallowed. My throat was tight and closing rapidly. I wasn't sure how many more words I could get out before it slammed shut.

"Sweetie, listen to Mom! You need to show them that you don't have a weapon! That you're not a threat! Drop the ball, Gabby!"

I shifted slightly to better view my daughter's face. Clenched jaw. Puckered brow. The same look as Kasper whenever he tried to retrieve elusive words. My stomach fell. I understood—I wasn't witness to a fearful child. Gab was thinking, considering.

"I know what you want to do, baby!"

The first sign of movement: a small squeeze of the ball. Then a more intense compression, knuckles blanched by the effort. A long exhale. A slow-motion blink.

"We won't win that way!"

Abruptly, the hand relaxed and opened. The ball fell. The sight of it bouncing on the concrete path was sunlight upon my face. With arms held skyward, I hurried over and stood in front of my second child.

"Leave us," I muttered. "And we'll leave you."

The Homeland car remained still, noiseless but for a faint hum.

"All finished," I added. "Goodbye. See you later. Bye-bye."

A blink in this game of chicken. The vehicle eased out of the parking space and glided out of sight. I let my aching arms drop. They wrapped around my trembling daughter. Tao licked our shins, all the while keeping an eye on the ball several metres away.

"Your Kasper voice made them leave, Mom."

"I guess so."

"I'm sorry."

"It's okay."

"I'm so sorry."

"It's okay, my love."

"I wanted to throw it at them."

"I know you did."

"I wanted to throw it so bad."

"I know you did, baby."

"R-I-P-*aration, Mom."*

"One day, Gab. One day soon."

The same dream. The initial scene true to memory again.

They are at the lake. The sun shines down from a forever sky, and the water, though cool, is irresistible. The cedars lining the far bank shrug and nod in the gentle spring breeze. Tao, swimming with the fevered, near-frantic paddle innate to his breed, is in a moment of delicate balance: he is euphoric, playing with Family, surrounded by shrieks of delight, raw skin soothed by the lake's crisp touch; he is also anxious, the water is deep and he is adrift, unsure of where his feet can find solid ground again. As the current picks up, the delicate balance is disturbed. The pack climbs onto a pontoon twenty metres from the water's entry, first Girl then Man and Woman. Boy is last, but there is no concern—a vault out of the green wash and onto the feet without a hint of helping hand.

Tao is alone in the water.

In the true memory, he is not forgotten—Woman watches his feverish approach, then, at the cusp of the platform, she cradles his haunches to aid a scramble onto dry land. In this dream, it is not Woman lifting him from the lake. It is the stranger. Faceless again, but changed: no longer the ears left untouched, now the mouth. Tao yelps and barks, alerting Family to the shocking presence. They turn. Woman, Man and Girl are clones of the stranger. Boy, though, is the opposite; every feature accounted for with the exception of the mouth.

Family and Stranger start to shout. The words are unrecognizable, but the tone is pure accusation. Boy, unable to join the chorus, conjures a set of headphones from the air and puts them to use. Tao jumps back into the lake. His desperate paddling starts to falter. Water enters his mouth, throat, lungs. He sinks, the darkness enveloping him. Stars of sunlight on the surface of the lake flicker, then wink into nothing.

The shouting follows him all the way down.

*

Tao squints, adjusting to daylight. He shakes his head. The commotion of the dream—has it followed him into the waking world? He hears only the creaks and sighs of the RV, the window curtains shimmying in a westerly.

He stretches and sits up. Scratches his chin. He takes inventory of his body. The long rest has helped. His skin is placid. Head, neck and back are mostly pain free. The busted leg remains a tight fist, swollen and numb, but no worse. The blood is congealed where the weapon rubbed the skin raw.

Boy is at the table, wearing the pyjamas found last night, eating the same snack as yesterday, or perhaps a new one similar in look and smell. Tao is surprised to find he isn't hungry. Still, he makes a half-hearted effort to beg. Boy shakes his head and holds the snack out of reach. No matter. All going to plan, they will reach the training site before sundown—there he will eat again.

Time to go.

He listens to the sparse sounds of isolation. Are the hounds waiting for them in their silent machines? He sniffs the air, alert for the sour and acrid clues of their presence. Nothing. The only addition to the salt and metal and smoke: a dash of petrichor from last night's rain. Nails clicking on the laminate, he walks over and stands by the door.

*

Kasper drops the last of the snack in the chest pocket of the pyjama shirt. Then he rolls up the cuffs on the pants to just above the ankles. The new clothes are annoying—too long in the arms and the legs. His own gear, though, is still wet, still in a pile.

Kasper notes Tao's position at the door as he reluctantly puts on his damp shoes and socks. He slips the headphones over his neck then tucks *The Gingerbread Man* into the back of his pants. The elastic is firm enough to hold the book in place. He walks over on tiptoe and stands in front of the dog. He reaches out with a tentative hand and pats Tao's head as if testing the heat of a cooktop.

"Goo'boy."

He steps past the dog and into the cab. Then he sits down in the driver's seat and leans forward over the steering wheel, placing his forehead against the windshield.

*

Tao stares at Boy, the door, back at Boy. He sits. He is beginning to understand now: the distractions are inevitable, but in the end they bow to trust. Granted time and space, Boy will eventually follow. And in a moment of concern or danger, Boy has enough instinct to run, especially when chasing the book. It is a different way of functioning in the world. But that is Boy: different.

Tao drops down onto his belly, head between his paws. He will wait. And trust.

*

Kasper sits back. He places his hands on the wheel—just the palms, no fingers—and scans the dash. With squinting eyes, he adjusts the rearview mirror.

"The old man, the old woman, the little boy, the spotty dog, the hunree crow all chase the Ginnerbread Man."

He leans left and presses his nose to the window, considering the poor state of the side mirror. He pushes a button on the armrest—the mirror doesn't move. He closes one eye and pushes the button again. No response.

"Oh nooo. Broken. Oh deeear."

Kasper climbs out of the seat and exits the cab. He bypasses Tao a second time and walks to the rear of the RV. With a hand up to shield his eyes from the glare, he closes the curtains on the back window. Then he applauds and joins the dog by the door.

*

Tao stands, tail wagging. He sniffs a pant leg, licks a sneaker. It feels good knowing Boy is not a complete mystery. And a seed of affection is planted in his garden of duty.

*

Their exit from the RV is uneventful. Arsenault Drive is clear to the north where it changes to Sixty-Third Street. Behind them the carcass of Gilder slips further into decay, carrion for the gulls and the crows and the official newsfeeds on the other side of the continent. Ahead the countryside unfurls, the brown land streaked grey like the cropped hair of a trauma victim. The overnight downpour has enlivened only the street—the asphalt glistens in the morning sunshine. Everything else is gunk and sludge and sickly mud and sluiced tallow. Oily rainbows peer out of the puddles.

*

At a property that a decade ago had sold its own butchered beef, they encounter a scarecrow. The body and limbs are nondescript: overalls and a red flannel shirt stuffed with polyester and weeds and paint cans. The face, though, is unmistakable, courtesy of a photo nailed to the bucket head. The fault lines in the forehead, the washed-out pallor. The gritted teeth. The air of poisonous farce. Seen too many times to count on the TV at home, seen yesterday on the poster in the bus shelter.

Tao doesn't know how the face got there or for what purpose. He only knows that crossing the street is preferable to being near it.

*

Vulnerable now. Daytime. Flat ground and open spaces. Cornfields and vineyards that promised cover have been razed. Occasional houses and barns—like last night, Tao is wary of seeking refuge in their ominous confines.

They arrive at the rail-line overpass. Quicker to go over—nothing to negotiate other than a few chunks of concrete debris on the tarmac. The brief elevation, though, brings wide exposure and nowhere to run if trouble were to meet them halfway. They could skirt the overpass and cross the tracks; it would keep them at ground level and finding the road again would be easy. The downside? The mud, the holes, the bindweed, the bugs—heavy going for a dog with three legs and a human in pyjamas.

Tao decides to stay the course and commences the short climb. He moves steadily, splint tapping the asphalt like a metronome. His eyes are locked on the road but his head is on a swivel. He is attuned to Boy in back: the crunch of gravel under tiptoeing sneakers, the quiet swish of cotton pants, the froglike croaks from a pursed mouth, the constant drum of fingers on a thigh.

When he reaches the apex of the overpass, it is not his intention to stop. What he sees, though, demands a momentary pause.

*

Mount Ross, standing like a crowned monarch on the northeastern skyline. Beyond the border, 650 kilometres away. Clear and white, free of cloud. A vision realized from a painter's brush rather than geological activity.

A dormant volcano.

Fifty years before, the neighbouring peak of Mount Costigan erupted, wiping out kilometres of surroundings. Steam shot five thousand feet into the air. Ash was found on the car windshields of Gilder. Eighty-one people died. Said the photographer who recorded the event from a chartered plane: "Closest thing I'll ever see to hell on earth."

He didn't live long enough to witness the scene of today.

Mount Ross did. It watches from afar. Stoic, wise. Unflinching. Like the lessons of history.

*

They trudge the charred and leprous land. Bodies are more occasional than in the town. Two males, mouths stuffed with rags, lay near an overturned tractor. A woman is slumped over a fence like a saddle blanket. In the front yard of a storybook rancher, a corpse floats face down in a shallow grave half filled with water. On an instinctual level, Tao knows that out here in the farmlands fewer lives were lost because there were fewer lives to lose. Still, the long stretches without a wide berth and averted gaze and the whiff of rot give him a hopeful feeling. The closer they get to their destination, the less atrocity they will encounter. And in his empty shrunken guts he senses that when they walk through the front gate of the facility, death will have relinquished its hold altogether on the humans.

*

Rounding a slight bend on Sixty-Third, they come upon a surprise on the shoulder: a tennis ball. Tao sniffs, noses it back and forth. The bitter odours of the landscape are in the fibres, but so are those of a human hand and a dog's tongue. He is set to nose again when Boy reaches in, grabs hold of the ball and underhands it down the road.

"Fish, Tao! Fish!"

Tao obeys, more out of desire than duty. Carrying the ball the rest of the way—it will calm him, give him a measure of comfort. He summons a slow trot and retrieves the ball. Returning, he is ready to resume their journey. Boy has other ideas.

"Fish, Tao! Fish!"

Twice more the routine. On the third round, he is reduced to a walk. When he comes back, he will maintain a distance to ensure Boy understands: *We need to go now.* He descends into the shallow gully where the rolling ball left the road and digs around in the fescue. Finding the prize prompts an unbidden pang of sadness: Girl is gone. He won't see her anymore. They won't play together ever again. He recalls her face when winding up to pitch. Eyes wide. Nostrils flared. Tongue poking out the side of her mouth as if testing the direction of the wind. He never ran so fast as when he was retrieving for her. And her face when he returned—bursting with pride, radiating light and love. This is the image of Girl he wants as the fulcrum of his memories, not the one of her laid out on her bed, broken and desecrated, a trampled flower.

Making his way back, Tao's happy thoughts have bled into the present. He imagines Girl standing beside Boy. Talking, hands on hips. Laughing. Looking his way and waving. Filled with all of the joy he remembers.

He is mistaken. This is not a dream nor the mind playing pleasant tricks. He does not see Girl at all.

He sees an old woman.

The ball drops from his mouth.

*

"Donny Miles, you can hear me with those earmuffs on, yes? You remember me? I go to Gilder High with you. May? May Tomczak? You come to my science class once a week with a helper. You remember me, don't you?"

The boy looks at his right hand then runs his index finger over the lines in his left palm. The corners of his mouth curl. The shadow of a dimple appears in his right cheek.

"Ha! I see that smile! I knew you'd remember! Oh my, it's so good to see you, Donny. Can I give you a hug?"

May holds out her arms. Kasper rocks on his feet, back and forth from ball to heel.

"It's okay if you don't want to. I remember from class: you aren't big on being touched."

He takes three deep breaths and squints into the sun. Then he leans toward May with his shoulder. She does likewise, ensuring only the briefest contact.

"I needed that," she says, dabbing her eyes. "And this is your dog? That's quite the splint on his leg. Got a few red spots on the skin, too." She bends down and reaches out with a palm-down hand. "Hi there, fella. This is a bad time, isn't it?"

*

Tao stares, panting. A friendly stranger with a gesture of passivity—he's seen this before. Different circumstances, though. They're not trapped in a garage, desperate for a way out and a helping hand. And he's more cautious now, more wary of human duplicity. Wiser to the ways of this world.

He takes a single step forward.

The old woman's hand is small and dry and delicate. A band made of soft cloth wraps around her wrist, in the centre of the band sits a small stone. Farther up, the forearm is lean and smooth—its only blight a graze at the elbow. On her head, she wears a scarf that covers her hair, ears and neck, leaving only her lined face exposed.

Tao sits, sifting through the energy sensed. Kindness and virtue, but also something darker. Not anger, or hate. Something debilitating and insidious. A stalking presence that has her in retreat, backed into a corner.

*

"Does your dog have a name?"

Kasper blinks, then jumps on the spot. He fixes his gaze on the base of a downed hydro pole at the side of the road. May fronts him, keeping an arm's length of distance. Then she bends forward, ensuring she is adjacent to his line of sight.

"Donny, what is the name of your dog?"

"Dog."

He glances at her, expecting another question, more words. She doesn't speak. She waits.

"Tao. Dog name," he replies, scrunching his nose. "Tay-ohhh."

May smiles, nods and stands to her full five-five height. "A bit more time and space," she says. "I remember Ms. Eaton saying that to us in class." She looks around, then adjusts the band on her wrist. When she speaks again, her expression has changed, from one living in the moment to one longing for the past. "Are you and Tao out here on your own, Donny?"

No response. More time? Not this time.

"Your family…Where are they?"

"Bye-bye, family. Bye-bye Mommy, bye-bye Daddy, bye-bye Gabby. Byyyyye."

"I'm sorry. I don't want to upset you. Let's try a different question. Where are you going? Can you tell me that?"

"Tao help."

"Tao's helping you, yes. He's a good dog. Are you trying to get somewhere?"

"Tao help."

May nods and folds her arms. Then she picks up a stick by her feet and moves to the side of the road. She kneels on a dry section of the shoulder and gestures for Kasper to join her. He complies. She starts to draw in the dirt.

"I remember another thing from class: you learned better with pictures. So I'm going to make a little map for you."

*

Tao yawns. He doesn't like Boy sitting with the old woman. She talks almost as much as the stranger did. She is not the stranger (not yet—she still has a face), but she is a distraction. A powerful one. Boy may need a reminder of the task at hand.

The way ahead remains clear. No flashing lights or advancing sirens. A few flies buzz in the air, a pair of cockroaches scuttle along the ground. A long-abandoned plough rusts away in one of the barren fields. Fence palings scattered in the nearest rancher's yard resemble the picked-clean bones of a giant's feast. Tao moves in beside Boy and lays down, back legs tucked under his hips, ready to resume the journey at a second's notice.

He will wait.

And trust.

For now.

*

"Okay, this *X* is us here. About seven, eight hundred metres back up the drive, just before the train line, there's a tiny little store called Back Country where they sell their own produce. You probably didn't notice it because the Russians went and knocked it down. Anyway, following this long driveway behind where the store used to be, there's a house and a big yellow barn. Not much left of these either, but I'll draw them here."

Kasper gives three big nods and speaks in a high pitch. "Two house."

"You got it. Now, go a bit farther north, say sixty or seventy metres, there's a door in the ground. A hidden door. It's the entrance to a bomb shelter. The people inside have food and water, enough for a whole year. Electricity. A kitchen. Living room. Toilets." The woman draws a square marked with squiggly lines. "It even has a library."

Kasper retrieves his book from the back of his jeans and drops it in his lap. "Run, run … Fass as you can … You can't catch me …"

"I'm the Gingerbread Man! Yes! That's one of Ferdy's fav—" May's voice falters. She sucks in a jagged breath. Rubs her puffy eyes, adjusts her scarf. Swallows. A minute passes before she's ready to speak again. "Donny, I'd like to take you and Tao to the shelter."

She walks a few strides up the road then turns. She waves.

"Come with me?"

*

Tao gets to his feet, licks his chops. The old woman started to leave—a fine development—then she issued a command. Not just any command, the one that cannot be honoured. The one he was afraid of.

He looks up, anxious to see Boy's reaction.

*

Kasper frowns. He stands and slips the book back into his waistband. He takes the stick from the woman. He draws in the dirt.

A long tube.

An *X*.

Another house.

A plus sign.

He shakes his head. "No come, no thanks. Tao help."

He turns his back on May and faces the black ribbon of Sixty-Third Street unspooling across the dismal earth.

May paces back and forth. Draws more shapes in the dirt. Uses expansive hand gestures. She talks, allowing time and space.

"Come with me, Donny... I think this is the best thing for you and Tao... Yes, he is a good dog, a fine helper... But he can only do so much to protect you... The Russians are everywhere... You know me... You can trust me... You'll be safe at the shelter..."

May lapses into silence. She stares at the sun, assessing its position in the sky. She corrals a strand of white hair back beneath her scarf.

"You probably don't remember this," she says, wiping away the pictures in the dirt with her scuffed, block-heeled boot. "When we were in science one time, Ms. Eaton gave us a task sheet on astronomy.

Something about naming constellations. I was sitting in the next desk over and I saw you had your own sheet, one where you had to connect the dots on the Summer Triangle. You remember this, Donny? I remember you kept turning the sheet upside down and the helper got real frustrated until eventually she put one hand on the sheet to keep it right side up. You sort of had a confused look on your face, but you didn't get upset. You drew the lines, did the work, and the helper told you what a good job you'd done. I thought about it afterwards—Why did you want the sheet upside down? Just because? Or did you have a reason, one that made sense if you thought about it? Then it hit me: it was December. Winter. To see the Summer Triangle in winter you have to be in the southern hemisphere. And how does it look in the southern hemisphere? Upside down."

May considers the pictures Kasper drew in the dirt. She nods and pats the dog on the head.

"I don't think you and Tao are just out here wandering around. I think you have a plan, Donny. I think you know what you're doing."

She digs inside her jacket—brown leather, bomber style—and pulls out a pair of mirrored aviator shades. She puts them on and shoves her hands in the pockets of her jeans.

"You're headed north, yeah? Me too. Let's walk together awhile."

*

The old woman sets the pace, and progress is swift. It's clear to Tao she has purpose, she has a target. Could she also be going to the training site? She's headed the right way. Regardless of her destination, while their advance continues in this manner—fast, direct, free of disruption—he doesn't mind her presence. And if she suddenly changes, if she takes a detour or summons the hounds or her face disappears, there is no restraint preventing escape. They are free to run.

She is a good influence on Boy. There have been no delays since resuming the journey. When distraction threatened, her command to come produced a quick march, legs working long strides, arms swinging high and strong. When she speaks, the tics and the noises of Boy are lessened, sometimes absent altogether. On several occasions, Tao has observed eye contact.

*

"Just so you know," she says, stepping over a pothole, "I'm fine with you not wanting to come with me to the shelter. You've got to stick to your plan, yes? I understand that. And now that I think about it, they might not have let you in anyway." She stops, a foot on either side of the road's dividing line. "I know you're not waiting around to get picked up by the Russians. I just want you to know, that's what will happen if you stay with me."

May lifts her chin, clears her throat. Kasper glances at her and copies the guttural sound.

"I know what you're thinking: If you're so dangerous, May, then why am I here with you? Well, you're safe right now, Donny. I promise."

"Promise. Cross my art... Hop today..."

"Sure. Well, one out of two."

She pauses to cradle her head. When she drops her hands back down, both are tight fists, knuckles straining against the thin, papery skin.

"My daddy's farm is close to where I found you, just a block over on Sixty-Second. When the Russians took my family away I wasn't home—I was having a lesson. You been in a plane before, Donny?"

"I don't know how to swim. They will catch me and eat me."

"I see. It wasn't a swimming lesson—it was one on how to fly a plane. Not at Northport, though. Not up in the air. A class session. Learning from the beginner's manual. It was an underground lesson, a secret."

"Shh. Quiet."

"Yes, very hush-hush. It was my fourth secret lesson. After the curfew was put in place, Mommy arranged for me to keep seeing my instructor. She told me that with so many things getting taken away, she didn't want me to lose something I loved so much."

May removes her shades, wipes her eyes. She turns the sunglasses around to see her face in the mirrored lenses. Then she puts them on again.

"Mommy was supposed to give me a ride after the lesson. She never came. I walked home knowing what had happened. When I got there, the house was pretty much the same except for the messages in white paint on the walls. I got a bucket and a brush and the last bit of water from the tank and I scrubbed the walls. By the time they were clean, I had a plan: I had to find my family wherever they were, get them out, bring them to Northport, get in a plane and fly away." She lets the words float in the air. Then she laughs—a clipped, nervous snicker—and folds her arms. "I mean, are there even any planes left in the hangars? Working planes? And if there are, how can I be sure to get one that has the balance and fuel for four passengers? Not much of a plan, is it?"

"No much plant."

"You said it. If you've got a better one, please tell me."

Kasper pulls the headphone away from his right ear, lets it snap back.

"How about you, Tao?"

A few metres ahead, the dog stops and turns, ears at attention. He squats and pees.

"I'll stick with this one then. And it starts in—" She bites her lip and looks at the sun. "—about two hours."

*

May moves in front of Kasper and holds up a hand. He stops. From the corner of his eye, he stares at her boots.

"This is really important, Donny," she says. "So I want to give you as much time and space with this as possible." As before, she bends forward, loitering on the edges of Kasper's eyeline. "In a little while, we will arrive at the turnoff for Northport. That's where I need to go. The Russians are doing a patrol there every second day, right around thirteen hundred hours, one p.m. When they arrive today, I'll be waiting for them. And, like they did with my family, they'll take me away." She reaches for the boy's shoulder, hesitates, withdraws the hand. "You and Tao cannot be around when that happens. So, when we get to that turnoff for Northport, we will say goodbye."

May steps back, allowing the time and space promised. To their right, at the entrance to a rundown cattle yard, a variety of sounds fill the void: a gate yawning and groaning, roused by a sudden gust of wind; the *plink-plink-plink* of water dripping on metal; the soft drone of a hundred flies jockeying for position over an animal carcass.

"At the turnoff for Northport," she repeats, "we will say goodbye."

*

They walk together but apart, banded but without interaction. Beneath their feet, Sixty-Third slides due east, pointing toward Highway 8 and brushing by the northern tip of Tanner Bog. Ancient stories told of a subterranean river that bridged Gilder Strait with the bog, and of great red-eyed horn-tailed monsters that would pluck people from the surface and bury them deep in the peat. They cautioned sailors of the strait to respect the currents, lest they lose their way and end up a relic of the wetlands.

Today the bog smoulders, much of its 1,200 hectares torched on the whim of a madman. There are bodies in the peat. And the monsters are loose.

*

"I have to stop."

May moves to the shoulder and sits down on the ground, legs bent, forearms propped. She lets her head fall between her knees. Watching with squinted eyes, Kasper tiptoes back and forth across the tarmac. Tao investigates, circling, sniffing.

"Just need a couple of minutes."

Head still bowed, she presses her thumb on the stone in the middle of her wristband. After a few seconds, she releases and shakes out her hand.

"Dizzy. Used to be once or twice a month. Now it's every few hours."

She shifts her weight over her left hip and, with a heave, pivots onto all fours. A walk back of the hands sees her slowly bend at the torso and assume a kneeling position.

"Can't ask you to help me. I have to do it on my own."

She eases into a crouch start, thumbs the wristband stone one last time, then extends her arms to the side. On unsteady but stubborn legs, she gets to her feet.

"Let's go."

*

"I can't believe we saw each other again, Donny. Especially now, before I have to…" May trails off. "Do you think we were destined to meet? Or was it just blind luck?"

"Luck."

"You think so?"

"Think so."

She smiles and nods, then looks up. The gathering haze is soaking the sun blood orange. "Do you think we'll get lucky again?"

Kasper pats the tip of his nose then scratches his head.

"I think we will," she says. "I don't think we've used up all our luck."

*

They skirt a pickup, beached on concrete blocks.

Hood raised. Doors open. A gaping hole in the windshield, but no sign of any casualty.

*

"This morning, I wasn't sure I could go through with this, Donny. But then I saw you out here, still alive, making your way, honouring your family, sticking it to the Russians, refusing to give up. Wearing pyjamas like you're John Darling in *Peter Pan*. You've given me strength, Donny. You realize that? You've given me hope."

*

In the distance, a blue sign, growing larger with each step. Then it is legible. Beneath the scuffs and the scratches and the bullet holes are two white symbols: a plane in flight and an arrow pointing ahead.

*

"There's not a lot past Northport—the highway, the tunnel, then it's about five miles to the border. That's where you're going, yes? The border?"

"Tao help."

"Yes. He definitely looks like he knows the way." May kicks at a rock in her path. "Are you meeting anyone there?"

Kasper stops, bends down, adjusts the straps on his sneakers.

"Are you going to try the official checkpoint or are you going to sneak across?"

He clamps his hands on his headphones.

"Ah, too many questions, too many words." She curses under her breath, strikes her furrowed forehead with the butt of her palm. "I'm sorry." Her chin quivers. "I'm sorry. I really am."

"Ohhhh, so sad. Wahhhh. Wahhhh. Don' cry."

"I'll try not to." She dabs at her eyes with a sleeve. "You and Tao have a plan—I believe that. You don't have to tell me what it is. You don't have to prove it to me. As long as you know it, Donny, that's all that matters. But…you're here. *You're here*. Not missing. Not captured. You're right in front of me. You're alive. You're *real*. And I'm abandoning you. Turning my back on you to…"

She presses the stone on her wristband.

"Donny, please, *please*, you have to know this: under any other circumstances—*any* other circumstances—I wouldn't say goodbye. I mean, it's family. My family. They have to come first. If it was anyone else, I would stay with you, help you."

She stops; Kasper likewise. They stand side by side, one looking down the road, the other staring at the ground.

"Can you forgive me?"

Kasper blinks, closes one eye. He takes *The Gingerbread Man*, opens it and fans the pages before settling. He reads aloud.

"Run, run, fass as you can…You can't catch me…"

As quickly as the book was accessed, it is replaced. He nods twice, then marches forward. In his wake, the sobbing woman hustles to catch up.

*

Reaching the last blue sign before the Northport turnoff, May has recouped her poise. She pulls a thin notepad from her jeans pocket and flips it open.

"Docs—check; weight—check; brake—set; fuel—check."

She pauses, unsure of the happenings at her side.

"Rivets—check; trim tab—check; antennas—check."

She stops again, certain this time, confident she's not imagining things.

"Oil—check; propeller—check; landing lights—check..."

She fronts Kasper, hands on hips, a smile releasing the tension in her jaw.

"Donny, were you tapping your thigh to my pre-flight checklist?"

Kasper rubs his nose.

"And were you shaking your hips and shoulders? Dancing a little bit?"

He jumps on the spot, landing with arms extended and legs apart.

May applauds then mixes a slow handclap with her rundown: "Flaps—secure; throttle—open; ignition—on; radios—on... Elevators produce *pitch*... The rudder produces *yaw*... The ailerons produce *roll*..."

She turns and twists and stomps and kicks up the dirt. He bounces like a ripe cranberry. Tao, caught up in the moment, barks and darts in amongst their wheeling, whirling limbs.

The dance lasts until the last page of the notebook.

*

They stop at the intersection. The Northport sign—featuring a cartoon Cessna 172 banking right and waving—is spattered with white paint. The blacktop to the terminal is a straight quarter-mile stretch of jarring ruts flanked by dandelion and clover. In the field, the runways and gates are bare. Three of the five hangars remain standing; two have collapsed, giant pyres eager for the match. The radar head on top of the control tower is still.

May coughs, clears her throat.

"This is it," she says. "This is where we say goodbye."

She removes her shades and hangs them off of her shirt collar. Then she kneels and pets the sitting dog.

"Stick to your plan, Tao. And take care of him."

*

Her debilitation—it's obscured by fear now. And submission. Complete and immovable. Were the old woman to roll onto her back, she might never find her feet again.

Tao looks at her tired face, her sad eyes. There is no duplicity in her. No trick that would set the hounds upon them. There is only a weight, heavy, pitiless, one she keeps to herself rather than adding to his and Boy's burden. She is a friend. Proven. Trusted. And about to be gone.

Tao places a paw on her boot.

*

May kisses the dog's head and gets to her feet. She waves her hands in front of her eyes.

"You told me not to cry."

Kasper presses his palms to his headphones. Then he leans toward her with his shoulder. May does likewise. They touch. The contact lasts several seconds. Wiping her eyes, she picks up a stick and draws an upside-down Summer Triangle in the dirt.

"See you around, Donny."

Kasper frowns as she pivots to leave.

He turns to the whimpering dog.

*

Not the old woman walking away.

It is Girl.

Tao feels the tug of memory, urging him to run to her, but he knows he must stay. She has reached her destination. Her journey is over—his and Boy's has yet to be completed.

It was wonderful to see her again. A treat. He wishes he'd kept the tennis ball for their brief span together. One last time returning it to her would've been a moment to treasure.

*

A pair once more, they walk on, entering the final mile of Sixty-Third, Highway 8 in their sights.

Neither dog nor boy look back.

10

"Wait, wait, wait. Slow down, Jay. Tell me exactly what happened."

One hand held his head, the other cradled his ribs. He tried to slow his breathing but each exhale was hijacked by a gasp.

"They came to the school," he said. "They've been before—this was different. There were so many of them, armed to the teeth. They were taking dozens away. They took Beth."

I sagged, then sat on the couch. Tao laid his head on my knees and stared with the expression that was his standard these days: How can I help?

"They read the charges; all the while Beth is shouting over them. When they were done, they started moving forward to arrest her. That was when I… I… "

His harried stare drifted to the piano. Propped on the keys was a picture Kasper had done with his volunteer carer earlier in the week. A paint-by-numbers watercolour of a pine tree with a snow-capped mountain in the background.

"Spoke. I spoke as they took her. Shouted: 'This is a good person. She's done nothing wrong. Love is love. What gives you the right? You will be defeated. Then you will answer for your crimes.' I said so many things—I can't remember the half of it.

"They ignored me at first. But I wouldn't stop. Couldn't. Beth was yelling at me, telling me to shut up. When that didn't work, she started pleading with them: 'Don't listen to him. He's not worth it. He's got a disabled child. They're leaving the country.'"

He shuffled over like a sleepwalker and sat next to me. The hands in his lap trembled.

"I couldn't do it. I couldn't just sit there and not say a word."

He turned to me, cheeks burning, eyes wide and round as soup bowls.

"I think we should leave. Tonight."

I nodded. "Go get the bags out of storage. Tell Gabby to start packing. Just the important stuff."

"Kasper—what on earth do I say to him? How do I begin to explain this to him?"

"I'll talk to our boy. Go now. We need to hurry."

He stood and shook his head. "Christ, what have I done?"

"What had to be done." I cupped his face and kissed him. "Go now."

He ran down the corridor and took the stairs two at a time. I closed my eyes, got to my feet, then looked down at Tao. At some point in the clamour he'd retrieved his blue shark. The head and tail of the toy poked out of the sides of his mouth. I patted his head.

"I guess you're packed already, pup."

The duo warily treads the hellish strip. Tao stays closer to Boy than ever before, right alongside, brushing up against the leg every few steps as if Boy had recently lost his sight. Travelling Highway 8, Tao is alert, ready for ambush, for confrontation, the trip of the hair-trigger into fight or flight. That it doesn't occur is scant consolation. They are entering the throes of the journey now, the misery that was promised when they escaped the house. A reckoning looms, and it cannot be avoided. The hounds will have their say before all is said and done.

*

A sight on the median diverts Tao's focus. A van facing south. Familiar make and model. White. The dog sits, then digs at his ear with his front right paw. Perhaps Boy's disease of distraction is spreading. Tao glances at his companion—no impatience in the body, no concern in the face. Waiting and trusting as a good follower does.

Tao approaches, sniffing the air. He notes the busted headlight and the dent in the grille. And something else—a dark-grey sticky substance on the fender, its presence simultaneously attractive and repugnant. He limp-walks around to the driver-side door. Black daubs like ink blots mark a trail from the footboard to the window. Farther along, the body of the van is a constellation of bullet holes, the differing patterns suggesting more than one shooter, more than one gun.

The back is open. Tao considers Boy again, now on the shoulder, face directed toward the ground but eyes flicking between the van and the tarmac. Curiosity mixed with the composure now. Tao yawns.

I can't resist, Boy.

You know that feeling, don't you?

He inches toward the open rear door. He remembers what the inside of this van was like. Seats and benches. Rubber matting on the floor. Soft toys. Trainer and Assistant and two or three other dogs in their jackets. And a buzz, an energy that filled him up like nourishing food, though not for bones and sinew, for something way deeper that told him everything was just so and need never be different.

He pauses. Noises. A scratching of nails on carpet, then again on metal. There is a brief silence, then a moan that blurs the line between human and animal. In his gut, he knows that Trainer and Assistant and the dogs are at the site, awaiting his and Boy's arrival. But what if by some strange fate they are here in the van? Could they not be allies in resisting the hounds? Could they not help smooth the way to their refuge?

Tao starts forward again, placing one paw in front of the other. A second moan claws at his ears, its higher pitch pushing it to the edge of a scream. The door creaks open an inch further. He is a step away now. In spite of his doubt, regardless of the moan, he indulges the sequence of a dream: a cheerful greeting, he and Boy climbing in, pats, toys, the door shutting, the engine firing, driving away.

The end of being alone together and the start of a new family.

*

Kasper pivots. He jumps on the spot and lifts his arms over his head.

"Yesss!"

He starts marching down the highway, squinted gaze fixed upon the object of his desire.

*

Tao detects Boy's shift, watches the departure. He sits. To his left, the bottom corner of the door nestles at his ear like one of Girl's whispered secrets.

The scene he remembers from five years ago—he will never know if it was today's reality. And that is how it must be. Help cannot be expected, nor can it be hoped for. The duty to lead Boy is his and only his. As for the resumption of family—it is the prize, not the reprieve.

Tao turns away from the open door of the van and commences his hobbled chase.

*

A blanket hangs over a speed-limit sign. Kasper looks it up and down, studying the details. Sky blue. Pattern of rainbows and unicorns. No holes or burns or stains. With one eye closed, he walks around the sign. By the time he is back at the original vantage, Tao has found him and settled at his hip.

Kasper touches the fabric. Soft. He grasps a corner and brings it to his cheek. Different than his favourite brown blanket, but not in a bad way. He reaches up and starts pulling; as it comes away from the sign, he is careful to ensure it doesn't touch the ground. With the reverence of a priest donning the Easter stole, he wraps it around his neck and shoulders. Then he pats the dog on the head.

"Walking," he says.

*

A kilometre out from Rosamund Smith Tunnel, they notice changes in the grim landscape: vehicles, previously scattered like seed, are now orderly and forming a queue. Trunks filled to bursting and roof racks supporting tottery towers. Suitcases, coolers, clothes. Canned food, jugs of water. No bodies that they can see.

The changes are a warning: the unexpected lays in wait on the road ahead. But nothing can prepare them for the tunnel.

*

Humans crowding the walls on each side. Men, women, children. Alive, though in the broadest definition of the word. Many on the ground, a few on their feet milling about. They sleep on towels and wash in buckets and warm their hands over feeble fires. Read books and roll dice. Bounce infants in their arms. Pray to their gods on bended knee.

All are quiet.

At first, Tao doesn't understand the lack of vocalization. Passing through the dim wash of a candle, he sees the source of the silence: every human's mouth is taped over. He peers further into the poor light—the figures he can make out are all similarly gagged.

A stirring in his stomach—thankfully, there are no contents to evacuate. He suspects the hounds are responsible for this ghoulish theatre and immediately his suspicion is confirmed. An armed trio emerges from the crowd and falls in behind them, guns levelled.

He looks up at Boy. One hand over the eyes, peeking through the fingers. Other hand pinching the nose. Small squeaks caroming in the throat. Still moving forward, though. That's all they can do: move forward.

*

At the midpoint of the tunnel, a man drifts out of the awful milieu and eases in beside them, walking at the same steady pace. He is tall despite a hunched gait that gives the impression of a shorter man. He wears a flannel shirt, sweatpants and sandals. Aside from the tape on his mouth, his face is dominated by two recent-looking injuries: a burst blood vessel in the left eye and a gash on his chin. A grubby, makeshift sling supports his right arm.

*

Tao watches, waiting for eye contact from the stranger. It doesn't come. No interest in Boy either—all attention reserved for the tunnel. He wonders if this is a friend of the hounds, though the anxiety and uncertainty in the man's every pore suggests otherwise. Regardless, the extra presence does nothing to allay Tao's overall sense of dread.

*

As the party approaches the tunnel exit, a stopgap checkpoint takes shape. A series of pylons ends at a temporary marquee that houses tables and chairs, a pair of standing gas heaters, a mobile filing cabinet, half a dozen open cardboard boxes, a small refrigerator and a battery-powered generator. Behind the marquee, four Homeland vehicles barricade the road.

Nearing the checkpoint, the stranger quickens his stride, creating a small gap between himself and the new arrivals. In the rear, the armed guard doesn't react or respond to the change—they continue to tail Tao and Kasper. The stranger passes through the pylons and stops at the foremost table in the marquee. Seated there are two uniformed

Homeland officers. The female—ruddy face a mask of unblinking intensity—stabs at a tablet computer with her index finger; the male—sunglasses on, feet propped on the table—peels an apple with a Bowie knife. The stranger raises his uninjured arm in surrender, waiting for the signal. More than a minute later, the female officer, focus still on the screen, runs a thumbnail over her lips. The stranger nods, lowers his arm and in one swift motion, rips the tape off of his mouth.

*

"Thank you for permitting me to speak. I won't take up too much of your valuable time."

The female officer waves a dismissive hand. Her assistant continues the slow peel of his apple.

"I understand how things are, the way this works. And I don't want to cause trouble. But these new ones who just arrived—" the stranger glances over his shoulder at Kasper and Tao, "and there are more to come—I just think those of us who've been here awhile could get extra consideration. Maybe have a better chance of getting through."

The female sighs and moves the tablet aside. She places her forearms on the table and interlocks her fingers. "You don't like our system?"

"No, the system is … I just think it could be … tweaked … a bit."

"Tweaked."

"Yes."

"You mean altered to give you an advantage."

"I don't believe—"

"An unfair advantage."

The stranger wipes the sweat from his red, raw upper lip. "With all due respect, my family has been here three days now. There are people who've been waiting a week, since this checkpoint was set up. I'm only asking that this be taken into consideration."

"We do take that into consideration."

"You do?"

"Of course. The ones who've been here longest—it would be much easier just to get rid of you. Then we wouldn't have this mess, this backup. But we haven't gotten rid of you, have we? You're still here. You're even talking to me right now. I'd call that pretty considerate of us. You agree, partner?"

The male officer carves off the last of the apple peel and sets the naked fruit down on the table as if it were priceless art. He wipes the knife on his shirt sleeve and places it next to the apple.

*

Tao feels a tingle in his paws, his tail bowing between his legs. The tension between the stranger and the hounds—he can taste it on the back of his tongue. If it escalates, what do he and Boy do? Surely Trainer and the jacket will advise. Or perhaps not. Perhaps, surrounded on all sides, with no option to advance or retreat, they are finally on their own.

Tao swallows. These speculations cannot alter a hard truth: their running has ended. It is time to stay, to stand. Maybe to fall.

*

"What's your name?"

"My name is Harsh Dugar, ma'am."

"Harsh Dugar, like every Def snowflake, you believe you are entitled to preferential treatment. We don't share your view. We believe everyone is equal, everyone is the same. Just because you were here first, that doesn't mean you're special. We treat everyone fairly here at our little border checkpoint."

Face flushed, the man rubs the back of his neck. His hand shakes as he brings it down by his side. "Again, with all due respect, this is not a real border. This is just a roadblock you've randomly set up. You're not asking for anyone's passport or ID. The real border is five kilometres further nor—"

The male officer takes his feet off the table, stands, adjusts his utility belt. He picks up the apple. "I'll make you a deal, Harsh Do-Gooder, or whatever your name is. You let me shoot this here Mac off your head and I'll let you and your family through."

The man looks around. He coughs. "Excuse me?"

"I shoot the apple off your head; you and your filthy family can pass through. Simple."

"You're kidding." He shifts his open-mouthed gaze to the female officer. "He's kidding."

She shrugs and reaches for the tablet. "Only one way to find out."

The man closes his eyes, lets his head fall forward. He turns and looks at Kasper, the unspoken message: What has happened to our world?

*

Kasper covers his headphones with his hands. He zeroes in on the closest pylon: the flaking reflector panel, the black tire mark, the small chunk missing from the base. He wants the man to stop looking at him, but he can see with his peripheral vision that the man is afraid. More afraid than anyone he's ever seen on a *scared* picture card.

If he had a second blanket he would give it to the man.

*

The man turns back to the male officer. "What happens if I refuse?" he asks, his voice a mix of white noise and words.

"Nothing."

"Nothing?"

"You're free to go about your day."

The man bites his lip. He exhales, and his mouth, seemingly of its own volition, fashions the breath into a query. "Where?"

"Where what?

"Where would the shooting happen?"

"I was thinking right here."

"Could we go off to the side of the road, where my family couldn't see?"

"Gee, I really think the family should see this, Harsh."

"Please could we go to the side?"

"I don't think so."

The man ponders for a moment. "Are we talking a bow and arrow? Like William Tell?"

"Fucksakes man."

"Will you use a gun?"

"What is this—Sherwood Forest? Of course I'll use a gun. Jesus, make a goddamn decision, Harsh Do-Gooder. The clock is ticking."

The man pinches the bridge of his nose. His grimace morphs into a shout of frustration. "I think…"

"Yes?"

"I think I'll…"

"Go on."

"Say…"

"Please say yes. Please."

"No."

The male officer pounds a fist on the table and sits down. "I'm disappointed, Harsh. I didn't have you pegged as a coward." He shrugs. "Ah well, thanks for the visit."

The armed trio pushes past Tao and Kasper and grabs hold of the man, who has begun to weep. They cover his mouth with a new strip of tape, then escort him back into the tunnel.

*

The female officer waves. "Come."

Dog and boy step forward. The female officer doesn't acknowledge them. She scrolls the tablet screen for a time, then tugs on the sleeve of her counterpart, who's now eating the apple. "You seen what's happening south, Lou? Contact all across the city."

"Yeah?"

"Real action. Not this tunnel babysitting bullshit."

"We did get to scrub Gilder."

"True. Precious little combat in that, though." The female officer looks wistfully off to the side. "We gotta get away from this garbage detail."

"Patience, MJ. In the meantime, do your job."

She looks Kasper up and down, huffs, then commences the orientation for the newly arrived.

*

"By executive order of the President himself, Homeland Union Security Headquarters is entitled to establish citizen checkpoints wherever deemed necessary. This is an official checkpoint. The conditions of the checkpoint, as determined by Homeland Union Security, are as follows: authorized staff decide who clears the checkpoint each twenty-four-hour period. The criteria for clearance are confidential. To be eligible for clearance, an individual or family must be within the boundary of the Rosamund Smith Tunnel. To be eligible for clearance, the individual or family must wear Homeland-issued tape over the mouth. If chosen for clearance, the individual or family must cross on foot—no vehicle is permitted north of the tunnel. These conditions are subject to change at any time. No correspondence or discussion on these conditions will be entered into, unless authorized by Homeland Union Security staff.

"Before we gag you, do you have any questions?"

*

Kasper shifts the blanket from over his shoulders to around his neck. He lifts *The Gingerbread Man* from the back of his pants and opens to a dog-eared page. While reading aloud, he chews on the nail of his right thumb. "The cunning fox said in a soo thing voice…

"Don't worry, I am a very trong swimmer…

"Jump on my back and I will carry you cross."

The female officer eyes the boy, brows high on her forehead. "Hey, Lou," she says. "This one's not right."

The male tosses the apple core at the back of a passing colleague, then leans forward in his chair. He removes his sunglasses.

"I'll be damned."

He whistles and clicks his fingers.

"Lieutenant! Sir! We have a couple of guests here you may be interested in!"

A man in combat fatigues hangs up a radio handset and strides over to the table. He is diminutive but muscular, back as straight as the yellow lines on the asphalt beneath his feet. His stout, triangular jaw is a cowcatcher fronting the train of his commanding features.

He listens to the murmured brief of the officer, then rounds the table.

*

Broad shoulders, barrel chest. Paws redolent of a black bear. A bite built to snap your neck. Teeth capable of grinding your bones to dust.

Tao whines. The formidable figure of this new hound is more than enough to leave him cowering on the ground. But there is more than an intimidating presence at work. There is history.

Blackened memories are stumbling into the light.

*

The lieutenant stands for a time, hands behind his back. Then he steps forward and places a hand on top of Kasper's open book. He pushes it lower, exposing the boy's frowning face and averted eyes. He nods as a smirk feathers his lips.

"Remember me?"

11

I sat beside Kasper on his bed. He was already anxious. Dad running back and forth past his door, Gabby dragging her suitcase into her room. He knew we were leaving in three weeks—he'd written it in his neat printing on the kitchen calendar we'd made from scrap paper. The frenzy of departure happening now didn't compute.

"Kasper, there's been a change of plans."

"No change!"

"I'm afraid so, my love."

"No change! Change is finished!"

I took hold of his hand then asked him to take a deep breath. He mimicked my puffed cheeks, my heaving chest.

"We're leaving tonight. This place is not safe anymore."

"Oh dear!"

"We need to pack up all your favourite things." I flipped open the lid of the suitcase at the foot of the bed. "I'll help you."

Kasper threw himself on the floor, his cries of "No help! No help!" like slaps upside my head.

"Shall we go downstairs and look at the calendar together? You can fix it up. Cross out the Goodbye *on the other date and write it in for today."*

"No no no no NO!"

"Would you like to hang for a bit? Help you feel better?"

"Feel better."

To my surprise, Kasper responded, lifting himself onto all fours and crawling over to the hammock. He wriggled his way inside and was soon swallowed up by the blue folds. I waited for the sign of self-regulation—on this occasion, a quiet hum of "What's Going On"—then exited to deliver my progress report.

"De-stressing in the hammock," I told Jay as he stuffed socks into the front pouch of an overnighter. "Didn't have to use Gingerbread Man.*" I patted Tao—he was curled up on his corner bed, blue shark in his mouth. "That may change. We still have to exit the house."*

"The book always works."

"It might not be enough today. He's okay right now, but when the moment arrives? I think we'll have to take him kicking and screaming."

He wiped his brow as he zipped up the pouch. "It's hard on him, no doubt. But I'm glad he doesn't understand why this is happening."

I hastily gathered some essentials from storage: winter sweaters, birth certificates, baby photos. As I was carrying them out of the bedroom, a thump reverberated through the house. Fuck. Kasper was out of the hammock and throwing himself on the floor again. I dumped the essentials in the bathroom and stepped back into the corridor. A second thump, louder and deeper, like a depth charge beneath the foundation. I scrabbled for support from the nearest wall, vaguely aware of Tao scurrying by me and down the stairs, barking furiously. My stomach turned to water as the truth dawned. Not Kasper throwing himself down. Not our son's struggle. Not our beautiful boy's resistance.

The violence was at the front door.

Lungs sucked dry, I tried to shout. I couldn't.

My words were gone.

"Sir, do you think a gag is required? He's not much of a talker. Clearly he's a retard."

The lieutenant wheels around and delivers a jab that catches his target flush on the nose. The male officer yelps and staggers away, knocking his chair over in the process. Blood drips from the hands held to his face. The lieutenant clicks his fingers and points at a woman in the marquee wearing a red arm band.

"Livingstone, medical attention needed here."

The woman escorts the male officer to a small first-aid station positioned in front of the Homeland vehicles.

"A shame," says the lieutenant, wiping his knuckles with a handkerchief. "Lou had potential." He drops the handkerchief on the table and folds his arms. "Where were we?"

"You wanted to know if the boy remembered you, sir," replies the female officer.

The lieutenant nods. "He remembers me. I think the dog does as well."

*

The pack had stormed through the door. Tao snarled and barked, but he was outmatched. There were too many of them. They were overwhelming.

Tao recalls that the hound standing before him was the alpha at the head of the surging pack. For a brief second they had faced off, locked in a stalemate. Then the alpha was on the move. It was beneath him to bother with the lowest rank in Family. He had more important battles to wage.

He was first to climb the stairs.

*

"Can you hear me with those headphones on? What's your name, my friend?"

"Friend."

"Hearing is fine. What is your name?"

"Name."

"Your name—what is it?"

"He reach a river bang. And the water seem quite deep."

The lieutenant turns to the female officer. "The simplest request." He shakes his head and focuses back on Kasper, noting his attire. "For the sake of this ... conversation, I'll call you PJ."

Kasper closes the book and holds it against his chest. He stares at a red sweetgum leaf on the ground.

"You don't really know how it played out, do you PJ? You were in that hammock the whole time. Now, if someone else was standing here—someone who had no clue about your condition—they wouldn't bother talking to you. But because I know this disease very well—and yes, it *is* a disease, PJ, no matter what the Def quacks say—I'm going to treat you with the respect no one else would give you, including your parents if they were still around.

"I'm going to give you a brief account of what happened."

*

Tao cocks his head to one side. He didn't think the hound would want to talk. And the tone of familiarity, even friendliness—unexpected. He scratches his ear. What is being said? Is the hound sorry for what he did? Is he explaining why Boy was not killed with the rest of Family? Is he telling Boy to end their journey, to stop seeking refuge and return to the house?

Soon enough, the words will cease and actions will commence. When that tipping point is reached, he hopes he is ready.

*

"We busted in and the mutt here was waiting. Commander-in-Chief doesn't like us shooting dogs—he's got a thing about it—so we stuck him instead. We went up to the second floor. Your mother and father met us at the top of the stairs; both had some sort of metal bar, a curtain rod or something. Not a decent weapon. We overpowered them and killed them. Laid them on the bed. Much easier for the baggers to lift them from a bed than the floor. They went down swinging, your parents—I'll give them that. Your sister too. Feisty girl."

The lieutenant lifts a cigarette out of his breast pocket.

"Your parents fought hard for you at the end, PJ."

He accepts a light from the female officer.

"What I don't understand, what I can't even begin to fathom ... Why didn't they fight just as hard for you from the beginning?"

*

The jacket finds him.

It is not the same as before.

The material is coarse, thin. It feels to Tao as though it could tear with a sudden movement. The fit is poor; the collar bunches under his neck, the trim sags beneath his ribs. He feels the tickle of loose threads.

Tao is grappling with the shift when Trainer murmurs in his ear.

Ignore your learning
And access the submissive
The supplicant
The animal that survives only
Because of human sympathy

*

"Corporal Davis, do you know I have a son not unlike our friend PJ here?"

The female officer sits up a little straighter. The tablet is switched off and out of arm's reach. "I was not aware of that, sir."

"It's true. I don't often talk about it. When my wife and I heard the diagnosis, we refused to accept it. I tore the paper up and threw it on the fire. We were at war from that moment forward. Hard work, strategy and sacrifice—that's what it was going to take to defeat the enemy. But we would prevail. We would cure our boy." The lieutenant drops his cigarette, crushes it with his boot. "Our son has made excellent strides. He graduated high school. His IQ has increased fifteen points. He has a vocabulary of five hundred words. He doesn't rock or flap his hands or walk on his toes anymore. We have channelled his aggression into useful avenues: boxing, wrestling, football. He is a citizen of this great nation now. He has a contribution to make, limited though it may be. That alone has been worth the sacrifice. And I have sacrificed, Corporal. I could've been a general. At least a colonel by now. I should be leading men into battle, not running a daycare for these ungrateful masses. But that is my cross to bear. God asked me to fight a different war. I fought. And I won."

*

Beg, Tao
That is my command
Beg
Not for food
Or water
Or a comforting touch
Beg for the boy, for you
For your lives

*

The lieutenant reaches out toward the boy's chest. He grasps *The Gingerbread Man* and pulls. Kasper resists. In the brief tug-of-war that ensues, the lieutenant is victorious. He places the book on the table.

"You're uncomfortable now, aren't you PJ? I can tell. Humming. Opening and closing your hands. Breathing fast. All because your book is on the table and not in your possession. Your precious book. A child's book." He places a hand under Kasper's chin and lifts, trying to force eye contact.

Kasper's gaze remains down and left, fixed on Tao's pink-brown nose.

"Your parents failed you, PJ. They didn't prepare you for the world. They didn't fight for you when you were a child, when it mattered most. They surrendered. And look what they made, look what you have become. A lost cause. A cautionary tale. For that alone, they deserved to die."

*

The book is on the table and Boy is suffering. Against his instinct, Tao ignores the problem. He can't afford to be distracted.

He begs, hungry for acknowledgement. An age ago he captured the hound's attention at the foot of the stairs, but he could not hold it, could not prevent the destruction of his world. Today, he must be an undeniable presence. Fail and there won't be blackened memories awaiting a future light. There will only be black.

Though his eyes are locked on the alpha, he senses a stirring in his surroundings. The painted lines on the asphalt bend and twist. Fog gathers in the marquee, obscuring all bar the front table. The table itself has turned bright white and wears a linen cloth that reaches the ground. The features of the female hound are fluid, forming and re-forming like clay on a potter's wheel.

No transformation for him with this worn iteration of the jacket. No doubling in size and strength, no cord to act as a tether, no swelling of the lungs to fuel a howl. Only his twitching nose.

He smells something in the hound. Something buried deep beneath the skin.

Something that could offer hope to Tao and Boy.

*

The lieutenant lets go of Kasper's chin. He puts his hands behind his back and starts to pace back and forth.

"When my men found you in the hammock, they wanted to kill you. I stopped them. I told them it wasn't your fault you'd ended up like this. You weren't responsible for your parents' failures. I told my men to leave you be. What I didn't tell them was that, for a fleeting moment, I considered taking you with me to give you a proper home. Maybe if you'd been younger, seven or eight. But at your age—What are you? Fifteen? Beyond a cure at fifteen, too far gone to be retrieved."

He stops and considers the desolate grey-brown landscape surrounding the mouth of the tunnel.

"I figured your fate should be left in God's hands, PJ. Me, of all people, I should've known: God's hands were already full."

*

The thing buried deep inside the alpha hound. Eating. Devouring. Tao can picture its origins. When it began feasting, the creature was smaller than a grain of rice. Now, it is the size of a cherry. It pushes forward, appetite insatiable. Soon, it will be behind his eyes.

Tao continues to stare, nose quivering. He and Boy are not the only ones begging to live.

The hound is too.

*

"We left you in the hammock, went back downstairs. Mutt here was done. We junked his leg to make sure. Then we moved on. Cleanup crew would be along sometime after that—I figured they'd pick you up. Or not. Either way, I wouldn't ever see you again." The lieutenant brings a hand up to the side of his face and gently massages a temple. "God has a plan. Before I leave this earth, He's given me a second chance to do His will, to do what I should've done."

*

Tao licks his chops, then opens his mouth, releasing his tongue. The intimidation in the hound's first impression—it is fading. The broad shoulders are now rounded, barrel chest sunken. The paws, though still large, have lost their claws. The carved jaw hangs limp as if broken or dislocated. The teeth are blunted and several are missing.

Tao watches, eyes not straying for a second.

I see it, hound. I smell it. I beg as you beg. Grant us passage and the creature in your head will stop feeding. Send us on our way and your plea will be answered.

*

The lieutenant joins his hands, bows his head. "Lord Almighty, give me the strength to do Your will." He performs a sign of the cross then returns to a feet-apart, arms-folded military stance. "PJ, your dog is really something. Survived the needle, got you here. Now he's staring at me, hasn't stopped since we started. What's your deal, mutt? I've got no food if that's what you're after. Or are you still pissed at us for sticking you and junking your leg? Come on, let it go. You're alive. And somebody made a fine splint for you—I know it wasn't PJ here." He clicks his fingers to the side of Tao. "Won't look away for anything. I wish my men had your laser focus, mutt."

*

He knows you see it, Tao
The sadness
The anger
The fear
All of it
Don't stop staring
Don't stop seeing
Don't stop begging

The mutating surroundings continue to grow. The lines on the road have paired up, forming a trio of crosses. The gathered fog has thickened and carries the scent of pine needles. The clothed white table dazzles like a dwarf star. The face of the female hound has settled—the sharp nose, pale lips and prominent cheekbones belong to someone new.

Tao remains stock-still, the threadbare jacket thinner than gossamer on his back. He feels the changes.

And more.

Something is happening to Boy, something brought on by his discovery of the feeding creature. And behind him, there is a restlessness in the tunnel, as if a thousand heads turned at once to observe the scene at the exit.

*

The lieutenant picks up *The Gingerbread Man,* taps the cover with the knuckle of his index finger.

"My son liked this when he was young. Most books wouldn't hold his attention, but this one did. We always had to finish it before the end, before the Gingerbread Man got eaten. He didn't like the way the fox was drawn in the pictures, as if he was the bad guy." He opens the book and thumbs through the pages. "When I meet God Almighty, PJ, He will ask me about this moment. Was I selfish? Did I learn from my previous mistake? Did I let you get on the fox's back when I knew what would happen?" With a grunt, he closes the book, hands it over. "You should have this."

Kasper holds *The Gingerbread Man* to his chest then lifts it up to his face. "Deep breaf... ihhhh, ahhhh... Deep breaf... ihhhh, ahhhh... Deep breaf... ihhhh, ahhhh..."

The lieutenant removes his pistol from its holster. He takes aim at the back cover of the book. "Goodbye, PJ."

12

I rose from the bed and surveyed the aftermath.

The room was wrecked. Not a sound though. Or maybe I couldn't hear anymore? Or smell or touch or taste? Maybe all you were left with in death was sight. And hindsight. Who knew? Not me. I was a newborn. I didn't know how any of this worked.

Jay was laid out on the bed. It hurt seeing him so empty, but the pain was more silhouette than substance, the long shadow cast by the memory of love. I asked him to rise, to join me. No response. I wondered if he was elsewhere. Anywhere. I grasped his hand and kissed his lips. No smell or touch or taste. The vaguest sense of déjà vu—that was all.

I drifted into our girl's room. Our girl. The words still had meaning. For now. Kneeling beside Gab, I remembered what I would've done in the previous world. I held her and I cried and I wailed and I curled up on the floor. When it was over, she faded into nothing like a breath on the cold morning air.

Then, our boy. Different, as always, but never like this. I knew he had survived when I saw the hammock—it was draped in a shimmering veil that I intuitively understood was the domain of the living. For the first time since crossing over, there were tiny kernels of raw emotion accompanying my sight.

Surprise.

Delight.

Fear.

Despair.

And want. Wanting him with me, but not here. Wanting him alive, but not in the world left behind.

Pebbles of feelings—I rolled them around in my hand until a new understanding saw them dissolve.

Another living presence.

Coming up the stairs.

Tao sees the weapon trained on Boy. His hackles rise. His muscles coil, primed for the leap. Everything tells him to act.

Everything but Trainer.

Stay, Tao

Look elsewhere now

Around

At the boy

Trust that your begging

Will result in clemency

Not extinction

Fighting the urge to strike, Tao drops his head and peeks over his shoulder. Humans have gathered behind him and Boy. Dozens. Hundreds. All are watching the scene play out at the table. They are silent, but by choice—there is no tape over their mouths. Their hands cover their ears.

He turns to Boy. A changed face, no longer identifiable. Broader than before. Nose flatter and slightly bent. A scar above the left brow. Strong jaw ending at a pointed chin.

Tao cannot name the stranger's mask that Boy wears. But the maker is obvious.

Boy is the child of the alpha hound.

*

The lieutenant curses and lowers the gun. He replaces it in the holster. For a second time, he reaches out and pushes the book down so that he can see the boy's face. "Run, run, PJ." He stands aside, arm extended.

Kasper takes a step forward, hesitates.

"Go on." The lieutenant nods and points at the dog. "Take the fox with you. He's not a bad guy."

*

Tao hears it: the command to move. He obeys, slowly rounding the luminescent table, ensuring contact with Boy's leg is not lost for a second. The alpha watches. So does the female hound. Neither seeks to stop the advance. Their energy is calm.

The fog clears as they make their way through the marquee. A few hounds glance, most are disinterested. None approach. None rebuke him for the flicker at the tip of his tail—the lone outward sign of the cautious delight flooding his body. He looks up at Boy. Recognizable again. Mask of the hound's child gone, book tucked away. A corner of the blanket has fallen across the right shoulder. Fingertips drum the left thigh with a nearly imperceptible beat.

As Tao passes the Homeland vehicles, the first piece of the jacket slides off and falls to the ground. By the first speed-limit sign on the highway, Tao is unclothed.

*

At the tunnel, a crash of noise like a tidal wave pounding a jetty. Shots fired. Shouts and screams. A squall of sirens.

Half a kilometre to the north, dog and boy march onward, each stride distancing them from the deadly skirmish.

*

Tao sets a pace quicker than at any other time of the journey.

They are unstoppable now. The alpha taking pity on them and allowing passage—it has blunted the sword hanging over their heads. No more hounds. No more flashing lights. No more sirens. No more perilous silences.

Other challenges could arise—strays, strangers, rogue packs, thunderstorms—but they are as unlikely as Boy finding a proper voice. And they have seen it all before. Seen it, met it and prevailed. They are free now. Soon Tao will be with an old family turned new, safe from the chaos, enjoying the rewards of duty fulfilled.

Boy feels good too. The bobbing up and down of the head. The upward curl at the corners of the mouth. The lifting the blanket high like a kite to let it catch a gust of wind.

*

They leave Highway 8 at the Dufresne Road turnoff and head due east. In this stretch there are tokens of civilization and little evidence of its breakdown. The asphalt is free of debris. The three ranchers they come upon are unmolested. The farmland is healthier here than south of the tunnel: copses of larch and fir abound and swaths of green invigorate the grey-brown dirge. One of the fields resembles a gridiron, marked by row after row of rhubarb. There are no bodies. An observer could be convinced the world wasn't doomed.

The normalcy is not lost on Tao. He sees it as a sign. More than a sign—an affirmation. The decision to guide Boy to the training centre was the right one, as he knew it to be when Trainer first tasked him with the delivery. Now they are within reach of it. He is tempted to move even quicker but suspects his injured leg is at full capacity.

A solid window of daylight is available for the final stretch. Much of the earlier haze has cleared, leaving an undiluted mid-afternoon sun to sail along its western arc. A smattering of clouds cottontail the sky. The breeze meanders down Dufresne, presenting to the duo the slightest of headwinds. The temperature is warm for early October.

At their current pace, they will reach the training site within two hours.

*

At a small dip in Dufresne Road, a waft of lavender sparks an association.

Woman.

Tao summons his most potent memory of her—the occasion when she thought he would die. It was early in their relationship; he had been dismissed from training and his permanent stay as a pet had just begun. Left alone and unrestrained by Family, he was free to explore the house in its entirety. Initially, he didn't move from his spot: on the mat by the front door, red toy bone by his side. The new reality was disorienting, scary. For consolation, he turned to base instinct.

The first goods he ate were within easy reach. Then he pulled items down from the dining table and the kitchen counter. He knew he was being bad, but how to stop when you've abandoned reason and surrendered to your appetites? He went upstairs, finding exotic treats in the bedrooms and the bathroom. When the hunt was complete—a good thirty minutes after his first kill: a bag of six bread rolls—he returned to the mat and lay on his side. He didn't feel better, but he was no longer empty.

The response from Family was predictable: shock and anger, mostly from Man. Then it settled. Then there were smiles. It was during the first bout of laughter that he began to feel ill. Woman recognized it immediately: "Pup, your hind legs. You're shaking."

She bundled him into the back of a car and drove at breakneck speed to the pet hospital. From the urgency and fear in her energy, he understood it was serious. That assessment was confirmed when he was prodded and poked in Emergency.

"Not a lot we can do with xylitol. Just charcoal and fluids. Hope and pray he's big enough to withstand it."

It was strange—in Woman's care, despite the newness of their connection, he never thought he would die. Something about her made him believe he would always be looked after when she was around.

Here on Dufresne Road, nearing the goal of refuge for him and Boy, Tao feels the same security. He detects her presence, not just in a scent on the breeze but in the grass, the trees, the shape of the clouds, the warmth of the sun. Woman is everywhere. She is with him.

Or maybe his mind is embellishing, lost in the reverie of a mission accomplished.

They arrive at their final deviation: a left at the intersection of Dufresne and Swan. Tao takes the turn, absorbing the view of the home stretch. It seems long. It isn't. Merely an afternoon walk. He takes brief stock of his physical condition; with the end nigh, he can afford to listen to his body again. It tells a tragic story. His insides are splintered wood. The worn patches of skin on his paws are darkening, turning black. His injured leg is so lacking in sensation he is surprised to find it still bound to his body. He is running on fumes. His body is on the verge of collapse.

A rest seems ludicrous given they are so close, but what harm could it do? He's not the only one who could use a spell. Boy is ten metres back, still standing at the intersection, deep in thought. Assessing the physical toll too? Thinking about Woman?

Tao sits. He can accept one final distraction. The way is their friend now, destiny their running mate. He eases onto his belly, front legs extended. Stretches and yawns. Rolling over onto his side, he is tempted to doze.

*

Kasper jumps on the spot then adjusts the straps on his sneakers. Searching around, he finds a stick in the fescue. He grasps it and sits on the ground. From memory, he draws the sequence of pictures:

A house.

Trees.

Lines. Up, down, across.

Two bumps.

A clover leaf.

A long tube.

A *T*.

A house with a plus sign.

*

Tao blinks.

Once.

Twice.

Third time, his eyes remain shut.

*

Kasper nods and throws the stick back into the brush.

He gets to his feet. The sight of Tao lying motionless in the middle of the road is worrisome, but he can see breathing, the chest's rise and fall. He taps his headphones then turns his back on the napping dog to face south.

He starts to walk, glancing over his shoulder as he goes.

*

Tao opens his eyes and scrambles to his feet. Boy is not at the intersection. Panic skewers him like a pitchfork. Gone? Can't be. Not an absconder. Doesn't leave without Family. I am Boy's only Family. I have Boy's trust.

Then he sees. Boy is a small distance away, heading in the direction opposite to their intended route. He barks and starts to limp-run. Then stops.

Boy pauses and turns. The direct stare is unlike anything Tao has witnessed before. And the voice. Measured, stern. The sort that it is unwise to refuse.

"Tao, come!"

Come? For what purpose? Tao scratches under his chin. It must be something Boy wishes him to see, something at the side of the road, or in the nearby field. That promised final distraction.

The voice, though. The tone. Rooted in importance rather than whimsy. If he hadn't heard it from Boy's own mouth, he wouldn't have believed it.

Tao obeys and wanders over. He sits by Boy's feet.

I am here—What is it you want me to see?

*

Kasper nods. "Goo'dog."

He takes a dozen more strides down the south road then turns again. He waves a hand. "Tao, come!"

*

Not a rest. Not distraction. Boy is leaving. And commanding him to follow. Tao shakes his head, causing spittle to fly. A dream? Is he still dozing on the asphalt? No, this is a waking nightmare.

Trust is all Boy has had to go by on this journey; understanding the mission, knowledge of the destination—they were mysteries. As such,

Boy can be forgiven for not knowing better. But regardless, this command is nonsense.

Tao backtracks to the intersection.

*

Dog and boy stand at twenty paces, sizing each other up like Old West gunfighters, neither willing to draw. Tao is belly down on the tarmac, weight leaning away from his harnessed leg. His scrutiny is dour and unflinching. Kasper's gaze is no less committed, though he has settled back into his standard: keen observation from the corner of his eye.

Ten minutes into the standoff, the dog gets to his feet and walks farther north, increasing the gap between the pair to Olympic-pool distance. He stops, waits. No reaction. He turns north again and tacks on a dozen steps. The result is the same. Three more times Tao baits Kasper to follow. Finally, on the sixth attempt, a reaction is provoked. The boy cups his hands around his mouth. Though the shout doesn't carry far, Tao can make out the words.

"Tao, come!"

The half hour mark. An upping of the ante. A tried-and-true method of persuasion that served Tao well in the early part of the journey. And with an added advantage: his actions will present as compliance, as if Boy has won the day. Not doing this at all would be his preference, but if the trust he earned is already lost?

Tao walks forward, head and tail appropriately low.

"Goo'boy!"

At Boy's feet, Tao drops onto his belly. He licks a sneaker then waits, hoping for the response he seeks.

No further prompting is needed.

*

Kasper bunches the blanket around his neck, lowers himself onto his knees and leans forward. With the open palm of his right hand, he pats Tao on the head.

"The Ginnerbread Man climb onto the cunning fox back…

"They begin cross the river..."

*

Tao jumps to his feet and darts in behind Boy. He latches onto the book with his teeth and drags it free of Boy's pants. There is a momentary scrabble on loose gravel then he lurches away. At the intersection, he drops the book and pivots.

Boy will be upset. Rightfully so—they were beyond this sort of underhanded thievery. The sense of betrayal will be apparent in the knitted brow, the high-pitched pleas. But there will also be concession, feet in motion and moving toward him, toward safety, toward destiny.

*

Kasper rises to standing, but does not move. His body shows signs of anxiety—twitching in the hips, the feet on tiptoe. His face, though, is resolute. So, too, the finger he points in the dog's direction.

"Tao, come!"

*

Tao paces back and forth, whining.

What has happened to you, Boy?

Has the loss of Family finally defeated you?

Do you now wish to die?

When he found the masters slain, he readied for the end. Then a new purpose was revealed and accepting death was out of the question. Boy feels devoid of purpose, but it is not true. Meaning waits with open arms at the training site. They just need to get there. By any means necessary.

Tao stops pacing and whining. He noses the book open. The smell of the pages engulfs him, filling his head like a balloon. On any other occasion, saliva would coat his tongue and drip from his jowls. Today, his mouth his dry. He places a paw on the book to hold it steady, then grips the corner of a page with his teeth. Several tugs see the page jerk free of the spine. He opens his jaws. The page catches a passing breath of wind, floats for a few seconds, then settles by a discarded plastic bottle at the side of the road.

He tears out another page. And another. He doesn't look at Boy—the briefest glance might send him mad. He tears and he waits. He will stop the second Boy's hand appears, not before. Pages dip and swirl and dance. And die. They sit on the blacktop in haphazard arrangement, like memorial plaques for the soon forgotten.

Then he is done. The book disembowelled, guts thrown far and wide, a grisly premeditated murder. Only the jacket and spine left to identify the victim.

Ashamed despite the necessity, hopeful despite the affront, he lifts his head and looks at Boy.

*

Kasper sniffs and rubs his nose. He checks his pants pockets for a tissue. Nothing. In the breast pocket, just the half-eaten snack. Only his shirt sleeve or the blanket to choose from. He chooses the blanket. The fleece is soft on his eyes but it spreads the tears around rather than soaking them up. After the last wipe, he checks the blanket. One of the unicorns is damp. He adjusts the position of the blanket on his neck and wipes his nose a second time.

Three deep breaths precede a wave.

"Tao, come!"

*

One hour has passed. Tao stares at the sky. He doesn't know how long he and Boy have been here but he sees the sun inching toward the horizon. And in the southeast a scrum of thunderheads has begun to form. He grunts. They can't still be here if there's a downpour. The deadlock must be broken before then.

Where are you Trainer? Where are you jacket?

I need you, now more than ever.

He knows they aren't coming; he knows they can't be summoned. Is it that they've served their purpose and the final challenge is his alone to best? Perhaps. Or is it that this last resort he is about to employ will disgrace everything they represent, everything they hold dear?

Boy is seated now, cross-legged on the road. Hands open in the lap, words dripping from the mouth like melted snow. Reading an imaginary book as if it were whole and real. Occasionally, a hand is lifted to wipe an eye. Tao wonders if Boy has an inkling of his last resort. The sitting position will certainly help in carrying out the foul deed.

No point in further delay. As he gets to his feet, he concedes: one way or another, this is the end. He walks forward, head down, tail between his legs. Each step echoes. The land holds its breath. He still senses Woman in his surroundings. Given what he is about to do, it is difficult to draw comfort from her presence.

*

Kasper tracks the dog's approach with his peripheral vision. He starts to hum the tune of "What's Going On," rubs his hands on his thighs and shoves his pretend copy of *The Gingerbread Man* into his waistband. He thinks about standing, then decides to stay seated. When Tao arrives, he reaches out.

"They reach the middle of the river."

*

Tao lunges forward and clamps his jaws onto Boy's forearm. He hears a yelp, a gasp. Shallow breaths. The thought of releasing the arm and biting just the shirt flashes through his mind. It's not enough. At this point of no return, obedience won't result from a tug on a sleeve or a cuff. Domination requires contact. Submission requires fear. He feels his teeth puncture the skin and sink into thin bands of muscle and tendon. He tastes blood on his tongue.

The breathing slows, deepens. No other sound. No movement. As it was with the book's destruction, Tao has tunnel vision; he doesn't dare sight Boy's face, a single glance will shatter his nerve. He sets his base and starts to lean back, bringing the arm with him. He notes the hand: open palm, splayed fingers. Not a closed fist. A good sign. He yanks twice, gentle enough to stop the flesh from tearing, hard enough to reinforce the new world order.

Then he lets go.

The arm withdraws to the midriff. The other slides under, cradling its counterpart like a sling. A thumb pokes at the spots of crimson dotting the shirt sleeve. The breathing now slowed to a near normal rate. He expected more than this. Much more. Anger, confusion. And the self-harm he assumed was inevitable. He anticipated a multitude of obstacles to overcome before Boy arrived at acceptance. Indeed, acceptance as the ultimate outcome was in no way guaranteed. Has he achieved it on the first attempt? Biting Boy is the worst thing he's ever done—doing it only once would be a tiny consolation.

He can make eye contact now. He must. To assure Boy it was necessary, to remind Boy he is protected, to confirm Boy's place as follower. He swallows, ridding his mouth of the taste of blood, and lifts his head.

The face Tao encounters is ready to end the impasse. In the half-closed eyes and the quivering chin and the thin-lipped smile, there is understanding: the bullets are spent, the chamber is empty.

It is time to go.

*

Kasper stands, wounded arm pressed against his chest. He moves ten metres farther south, then turns. His first attempt at speaking is scuttled by a cough. Second time, his voice is clear, assured.

"Tao, come."

*

The dog scratches at his ear, then his chin. He looks to the north. The road is endless now. He blinks, hoping a few last images of the site reach his mind's eye. None appear. Just a pall of black.

Yes, it is time to go.

Boy's home—that is their destination now. They won't find safety or refuge there, only oblivion. As it always was, as it always will be. Boy's home is chaos, anarchy, a place where purpose and duty are reserved for rituals and distractions and meaningless words. It is not Boy's fault—it is simply Boy's nature. In the end, it cannot be overcome by good intention or sad delusion. Were it otherwise, Tao would turn around, head north and never look back. His nature is to follow, to serve. To be lesser. As it turns out, lesser even than he imagined.

They are a lost cause. They were from the beginning.

Tao walks over and stands beside Boy. He sniffs the air. The lavender scent is gone, smothered by the stench of smoke and salt.

*

The pair begins their shuffle along Swan, headed south.

Two hundred metres out from the junction, Tao stumbles and falls. With Kasper's assistance, he resumes his feet. A few steps later, he falls again. Second time, he is unable to stand.

Within a minute, he has lost consciousness.

13

I watched Tao scrabble by the open door. He was enveloped in a glistening silver cloak—clearly alive. Just as obvious was the nasty injury to his back leg and the pronounced limp.

I wasn't the only one to notice.

Kasper peeked between the folds of the hammock in time to see pup pass by. Up to that moment, knowing my connection to the life before was dwindling, I'd been content for our boy to be shielded. He didn't need to see what had happened to us; he could stay in the hammock without the burden of witnessing that terrible scene. Indeed, he could close his eyes to the whole world: the demons in charge, the monsters on the street, the pain that couldn't be avoided, the suffering that might never end. And I would be here. For every second remaining that I could see him and recognize him and feel something that resembled my limitless love of the past, I would be right here. We could be together until the end of time, his or mine.

But now that Tao was alive and hurt, inaction was impossible. As Kasper settled back into the hammock, his stillness belied the frenzy of activity beneath the surface. In his heart, the joy of realizing he was not alone. In his gut, fear of the known and the unknown. In his mind, a map of the town and the place they must go. All of it driven by a duty he didn't know existed prior to pup limping past his door.

The end of time.

Mine.

I leaned into the hammock and kissed our boy on the forehead. No smell or touch or taste. I stood and looked around the room. A few objects caught my eye: a pair of yellow headphones, a brown blanket, a child's book. I wasn't sure why I lingered on these items, but I didn't reach for an explanation. As I crossed the threshold of the room, I looked back, viewing the hammock for the final time. At first glance, our boy hiding inside a blue teardrop, hoping never to be found.

Looks can be deceiving.

Death is strange.

The darkness was expected—everything else is cause for confusion. Footsteps. Laboured breaths. Occasional grunts. The smell of sweat and salt and a fruity something that reminds him of the sticks Girl often used to coat her lips. His body on hard ground, but cushioned by a thin layer of soft cloth. The feeling of being dragged along.

A voice.

Unfamiliar. Ominous.

"Stay right where you are."

Tao opens his eyes and squints. He is laying in the middle of an unfamiliar drive, on the blanket Boy found on the highway. He is positioned on his side, good hind leg bearing his lower body weight, bad leg and supporting splint pointing toward the setting sun. Past the tip of his tail, a corner of the blanket rises into the grasp of Boy's left hand. The knuckles of the hand are grazed and stained with dried blood.

"Empty your pockets, nice and slow."

Boy releases his grip and the blanket corner falls to the ground, permitting Tao full view of the scene. At the end of the drive is a two-storey structure that is more fortress than building. The windows are barricaded with metal shutters. Fronting the building is a primitive fence of concrete and corrugated iron. Barbed wire sits atop the fence. The gate is crowned by a series of rods with tips as sharp as spearheads.

A man stands at the entrance dressed in a green military uniform. He aims a gun at Boy. The aura about him is angry, dangerous, resentful of the world in which he resides.

A hound in human clothing?

"That dog you dragged here—he alive or dead?"

Tao sniffs and stretches his neck. Alive after all.

But not for much longer.

Boy has brought them here to die. The latest in a long line; so many lives have been lost in the building—he can sense it from afar. The anguished cries of humans and animals haunt the space like the last words of a condemned man.

"Start talking or keep walking."

He is ready, as he was thirty hours ago laying at the foot of the masters' bed. He bears no ill will toward Boy—their time together has knotted them in a way that won't be undone by their imminent demise. In fact, he feels something akin to love. Not the same adoration he felt for Woman, Man and Girl, but love nonetheless.

He recalls again their first meeting. Woman introducing them, cautioning Boy to be gentle. The approach, the low hum in the belly. The touch of his ear with the tip of an index finger. Then the leap back, looking at the finger through half-closed eyes, laughing. Boy was a riddle he couldn't solve in that first encounter. Not in the first month, not in five years under the same roof. Not on this journey, despite what he believed along the way. He will go to the eternal black without any real understanding of Boy.

But perhaps some humans were never meant to be understood.

"Easy, soldier. There's no threat."

A second voice. Tao lifts his head. A woman wearing a face mask and dressed in scrubs walks down the driveway. She pats the uniformed man on the shoulder, prompting a lowering of the gun. Then she opens the gate and approaches. She has dark skin and grey braided hair. Beneath the short sleeve of her shirt, her left arm is coarse and ridged, the result of a bad burn in childhood years. When she lowers the mask down to her neck, her freckled face is open, inviting. Apart from her place of origin—the feared building—nothing about her suggests a hound.

*

The woman looks Kasper up and down, noting the headphones, the tapping of the thigh, the averted eyes. The bite mark and blood on the forearm. She goes down on one knee for a closer look at the dog. The harnessed leg is her target—she lays a hand on the injured limb then gently presses the hip joint. Nodding, she resumes her feet. She mimes removing headphones; Kasper complies while staring at her slippered feet.

"My name is Kim," she says, patting her breast.

"Kim."

"That's right."

"My name isss Kasper."

"Pleasure to meet you, Kasper."

"Once upon a time live a little boy."

"I'm sorry."

"Live a little boy—sixty-eight treat. Gilder."

"You live ... in Gilder?"

"Sixty-eight treat."

Kim turns to her uniformed colleague, brow arched. "You've come a long way, Kasper. You and your dog."

"Tao-dog. *T-A-O* dog."

"Good name."

"Tao help. Kim, Tao help."

She nods. "I can help Tao, yes."

"We are at capacity, Doctor," interjects the soldier. "We have no space."

"We'll make space." She smiles at the boy. "Busy. We're a lot more than just an animal hospital these days." She picks up the lone item emptied from Kasper's pockets. "This all you had to eat?"

"No eat! Tao, no! No eeeeat!"

"You're right—Tao shouldn't have chocolate. Although this amount, his size ... He'd be okay if you had given him some."

"Tao, no eeeeat!"

"Absolutely, Kasper. Tao, no eat."

Kim signals in the direction of the building then turns back to Kasper. She folds her arms and nods. "Remarkable," she whispers. A minute later, two men in the green uniform emerge from the hospital entrance carrying a stretcher. As they hustle toward the gate, Kim folds down the collar of Kasper's pyjama shirt.

"You did amazing. Now it's our turn. We'll take good care of Tao."

The men lift the dog onto the stretcher, then listen to Kim's instructions: "Head-to-toe exam. Drip. Blood sample. Radiograph to confirm the harnessed leg is in the correct position. We're out of Novox so have some aspirin ready."

The men start to move, then stop as Tao raises his head. He barks, a feeble but urgent plea.

"What's wrong, pup? You want your blanket?"

Tao barks again, stronger this time. He paws at the edge of the stretcher. Kim turns, following his line of sight. Kasper, headphones attached, is walking down the driveway toward the road. He lifts a hand and waves. "Finish. Tao help, finish."

"Wait! Wait!"

Kim jogs to catch up.

"We can help you too. You don't have to leave."

Kasper rubs his eyes, his nose. His forearm aches—he would like to punch the bite mark, but he doesn't want to scare the woman. Instead, he shakes his wrist and jumps on the spot. Then he kneels by the side of the driveway.

"We'll make sure your arm is okay, make sure it heals up nice."

He draws in the dirt with his finger.

House with a plus sign.

T.

Vertical lines.

Stop sign.

Broken horizontal line.

The word *inspection*.

"We'll get something in your belly besides chocolate."

Kasper stares at the drawings, then closes one eye.

Kim examines the pictures in the dirt then presses her hands together.

"Inspection ... The border? Is that what you're thinking?"

She kneels beside the boy. When she speaks, she stares straight ahead.

"What you must have gone through to get here—I can't even begin to imagine. You're a survivor. And I want to respect that. I'm not going to force you to do anything you don't want to do."

She hikes a thumb over her shoulder.

"But you hear Tao, yeah? You hear him whining? He needs you. He needs his buddy."

She turns to Kasper. After a moment, she stands and extends a hand.

He wipes away the dirt drawings and gets to his feet. He touches the woman's outstretched hand with his pinkie. "Little boy wait by the oven for the Ginnerbread Man. He was very hunree."

"Hungry? Yes, absolutely. My treat."

Kasper nods three times and marches back up the driveway. He picks up the blanket, wraps it around his shoulders. Then he eases in beside the stretcher. With an open palm, he pats Tao on the head. "Goo'boy."

*

Inside the building is a hive of activity. People in green uniforms, faces sombre and full of intent, scurrying about, gathering supplies and filling backpacks, inspecting weapons of various descriptions. The hospital staff—outnumbered five to one—tend to patients, some human, some animal. At the end of a long hallway, the men transporting Tao branch off and pass through the swinging doors of an examination room.

"We can wait out here," says Kim. She ushers Kasper over to a nearby sink, gently lifts his blood-stained pyjama sleeve and washes the wound with soap and water. "You good?"

"Good."

"Don't mind me touching you?"

"Tok to meee, so you can seee, wuzz going on, right on baby."

She smears an ointment on the tooth marks and wraps the forearm in a bandage. Then she sits and pats the seat beside her. "Now, I promised you supper, didn't I?"

"He was very hunree."

"That's right, the little boy was waiting by the oven for the Gingerbread Man. Sadly, we only have MREs. Would you like the beef stew or the spaghetti?"

"Basketty."

"You got it."

While Kim is away, Kasper half closes his eyes and stares at the flag tacked to the opposite wall. It's the first time he's seen this flag without the splash of white paint.

"The Defiance banner," she says on her return. "The good guys."

"Good guys."

"The squad we've got here at the moment—they're leaving early in the morning to join the fight in the city. If they're as tough and resourceful as you, Kasper, we are sure to win." She hands over the meal. "Basketty, as ordered. You eat here while I go and check on Tao, okay?"

"Okay."

She smiles and winks. "I'll be back before you can say 'Run, run, as fast as you can.'"

As the woman walks through the swinging doors, Kasper lifts the plastic off of the dish and waves at the released steam with the back of his hand. He gives three big nods. "That was the end of the Ginnerbread Man."

EPILOGUE

The dream, for the last time.

They are at the lake. The sun shines down from a forever sky and the water, though cool, is irresistible. The cedars lining the far bank shrug and nod in the gentle spring breeze. Tao, swimming with the fevered, near-frantic paddle innate to his breed, is in a moment of delicate balance. He is euphoric, playing with Family, surrounded by shrieks of delight, raw skin soothed by the lake's crisp touch. He is also anxious; the water is deep and he is adrift, unsure of where his feet can find solid ground again. As the current picks up, the balance is disturbed. The pack climbs onto a pontoon twenty metres from the water's entry, first Girl, then Man and Woman. Boy is last, but there is no concern—a vault out of the green wash and onto the feet without a hint of helping hand.

Tao is alone in the water.

No matter how hard he swims, safety remains out of reach. He yelps and barks, hoping to alert Family to his struggle. Family, however, cannot respond. They are fading from sight like the ripples created by his paddling paws. First Woman, then Man, then Girl. Before long, only Boy is left on the pontoon. Headphones on. Humming a tune. Reading the book.

He knows how the dream goes: his desperate paddling falters; water enters his mouth, throat, lungs; he sinks, darkness enveloping him; stars on the surface of the lake flicker, then wink into nothing. But this is not the expected dream. In fact, this doesn't feel like a dream at all, rather something closer to memory. A hand grabs him by the scruff of the neck and hauls him from the depths. Before the idea of rescue has formed in his mind, he is set down on the pontoon. He shakes, then looks up. Boy still sports the headphones, still hums, still reads. But there is a change—the clothing. Familiar attire: a jacket, stone grey with royal blue trim.

They stand, side by side, facing the far bank, presence affirmed by the nod of the cedars, avowed by the beaming sun that shines upon their faces alone, together.

ACKNOWLEDGEMENTS

Bringing this novel to your hands, dear reader, required a tenacity Kasper and Tao would appreciate, and an army of allies to make the Homeland forces turn tail and run.

My heartfelt appreciation, as always, begins with my first reader and beautiful wife, Wendy—thank you for not divorcing me when you discovered I'd murdered a veiled version of our family in the opening chapters. Thank you to Chloe for being a kindred creative spirit, and to Jared for being the source of this work's wonder. Thank you to our much-loved, never-forgotten Tao for flubbing guide-dog training and becoming ours. Thank you to the Groth and Fraser clans for being awesome.

Thank you to Silas White, Emma Skagen and all at Nightwood Editions for your vision, your fortitude and for giving this story a fine home. Thank you to my agents: Tara Wynne at Curtis Brown Australia for still believing in me after all these years, and Olga Filina at 5 Otter Literary for expertly shepherding the publishing deal. Thank you to Kylie Ladd for assuring me this novel had the goods. Thank you to Emily Davis for sharing your experiences of learning to fly.

And thank you, dear reader, for giving this story a chance. I hope it connected in ways that will help you see the Kaspers of our world in a new light.

PHOTO CREDIT: CHLOE GROTH

ABOUT THE AUTHOR

Darren Groth is the author of seven novels including *Kindling* (Hachette Australia, 2010), *Are You Seeing Me?* (Orca, 2017), *Munro vs. the Coyote* (Orca, 2017) and *Infinite Blue* (Orca, 2018). He won the 2016 Adelaide Festival Award for Young Adult Literature and has been nominated for numerous other prestigious prizes, among them the Governor General's Literary Awards, the BC Book Prizes, the OLA White Pine Award, the CBCA Book of the Year (Australia) and the Prime Minister's Literary Awards (Australia). Groth is a passionate advocate for the representation of neurodiversity and intellectual disability in literature, and is the proud father of a son with autism spectrum disorder. When he's not watching *American Ninja Warrior* with his beautiful wife, he's eating Fatburger with his wondrous twins. He lives in Vancouver, BC.